#1 AMAZON BESTSELLER

AFTERMATH

FIVE MONTHS OF HELL BROUGHT TWO MEN TOGETHER

CARA DEE

ONE

_3 AM_

.

UNABLE TO SLEEP, Austin left the bed, slid on his new black-framed glasses, and trudged downstairs. It was August, and that meant the AC was working around the clock, but Austin still preferred the fresh air outside.

That could be considered ironic because Bakersfield topped many lists of cities where it was too polluted and dirty. But after having spent five months in a basement against his will, nothing was going to stop him from being outdoors.

Wearing only his sleep pants, he pushed open the patio door and slumped down in one of the chairs. Immediately he regretted not grabbing a glass of bourbon first, but he was too lazy to bother now. Instead he sat silently, absently massaging his bandaged wrists, and stared out at the backyard, only illuminated by the lights in the large swimming pool.

His wife's words were still wreaking havoc inside of him, and he suspected that was one of the reasons he couldn't sleep.

"We have to leave this behind us now, Austin. It's in the past. I miss you, and I want you back."

Jade, Austin's wife of fifteen years, wasn't a cruel woman; he wouldn't have stayed married to her if that were the case. But to say something like that... How did you simply leave a five-month long kidnapping behind you? How did you move on? How did you ignore a time in your life where you didn't know if you'd even live to see tomorrow?

He often tried to talk to her about it, but she wouldn't hear him out. She kept repeating her words about leaving the past in the past.

Scrubbing a hand over his jaw, he groaned and then rubbed his shoulder—the one that was still bothering him. It had been about a month now since he and another six men had returned to freedom, and he'd been poked and prodded by too many doctors to count.

His eyes were still sensitive to direct sunlight. His body was slowly healing after being beaten and broken in captivity. He had constant headaches, which only got worse with the new glasses he had to get used to. The dull ache in his ribs annoyed him. Scars now decorated his body, and he'd lost too much weight too quickly, so every meal now came with protein shake supplements along with the pain medication he'd been prescribed. There was also a physical therapist involved, as well as a psychologist specializing in trauma.

Yeah, let's just move on.

Austin snorted quietly to himself and leaned his head back, struggling with his anger.

Anger was new. He'd always been a quiet man, content to be content, and had never been demanding. But now? Christ, he was constantly on the verge of lashing out, especially when one of his headaches began to pound. During a few questionings by the police, and one particularly gruesome interview by a news reporter, Austin had stormed out before he could either do serious damage to furniture or rearrange a few faces.

Questions bothered him, because he didn't have concrete answers, so maybe his wife's request was good. Perhaps he could just let this die; he'd move on and pretend everything was all right.

I hear Santa's real, too.

"Daddy?"

Austin's head snapped around; he'd clearly been too deep into his thoughts to hear the patio door opening. "What're you doing up, baby girl?" he asked, clearing his throat. He waved her forward, his heart giving an extra thump at the sight of his ten-year-old. In captivity, he had missed her so much. Her hazel eyes, light brown hair, and heart-shaped face reminded him of what was worth fighting for.

"Can't sleep." Riley shrugged and padded over to him, hopping up to sit on her father's lap.

He was usually "Dad," but after coming back home, Riley had reverted to the little girl she once was in need of comfort. But you wouldn't find Austin complaining. He held his girl close and kissed the top of her head.

"Do I *have* to go to Nana and Pops' tomorrow?" she asked sullenly.

Austin cracked a small smile, although there really wasn't any humor in the situation. Riley adored Austin's parents—secretly a lot more than Gramma and Gramps on Jade's side—but nowadays, Riley was reluctant to leave his side.

It was a good thing it was summer break. Austin had a feeling it wouldn't have been easy to ship off Riley to school every morning.

"You know I won't be home, anyway," he murmured. "You'll have fun with Nana and Pops. I heard they're taking you to the zoo." He stifled a yawn, too tired for words, but knew his mind wouldn't let him fall asleep.

Another reason Austin couldn't sleep was his odd need to check in with Cam—the man he'd been thrown into a cage-like cell with all those months ago. After spending most of that time together, they'd formed a bond he didn't understand, but it was there nonetheless. In fact, it felt wrong not to see him every day now. Since they'd been returned to freedom, they'd only seen each other in passing, and Cam had called him yesterday and told him, *"Get your ass to my house."*

To an outsider, Cameron Nash was standoffish and almost appeared threatening. He looked like a bad boy, talked like he didn't give a rat's ass, and walked like someone you didn't want to meet in a dark alley. Not like he owned the world, but... more like, *"I fucking dare you to take one step closer."* But Austin knew better. He knew it was a shield Cam put up to defend himself.

"But you'll be home by dinner, right?" Riley's soft voice

brought Austin back once more.

"I promise." He gave her a squeeze.

Later, when he'd convinced Riley to go back to bed, Austin found himself dozing off in the chair on the patio, and the flashbacks and bad dreams followed quickly.

AFTER PAYING FOR the gas, Austin returned to his wife's Rover, eager to continue his day off. It had only been interrupted because Jade was going shopping later, and she hated having to stop for gas. Since Riley wanted ice cream, Austin had offered to step out for a bit to fill up the car and buy strawberry popsicles.

It was Saturday, and with the thermometer showing 89 degrees, it was a record-breaking day for early February. It meant Pool Day for the Huntleys. Well, at least for Austin and Riley. Jade didn't go near the pool until the weather had heated up the water a bit more.

Before Austin could close the car door behind himself, there was suddenly a hand shooting up. The stranger acted while Austin was in shock, and soon a cloth covered his nose and mouth. During a brief struggle, he inhaled sickeningly sweet vapors of something chemical through a gasp, which caused numbness to set in and his vision to blur. Only a few seconds later, he was unconscious.

When he woke up, not for the first time, he was dazed, nauseated, cuffed, confused, and he was enveloped in darkness. That was a first. The few times he'd woken up before, that meaty hand had reappeared and covered his mouth and nose again with the same cloth, and Austin hadn't been strong enough to fight. And it hadn't been dark. But now...

He looked around himself, panic creeping up his spine, but he saw nothing. Not even his hands that he could feel cuffed together in front of him. It was pitch-black, and as his senses slowly returned to him, he gagged at the smell of sweat, urine, and vomit.

"He-hello?" he croaked as a furious headache settled in. Judging by how his voice carried, he guessed he was in a small space.

Then there was a response. "Not your lucky day, man."

Fear shot through Austin, and he automatically pulled his legs closer to his body and raised his arms in case a fight was coming. He was definitely not alone in this small… wherever he was.

"Where am I?" Austin demanded in a rasp.

This time, the man spoke softer. "No idea."

TWO

AFTER HIS SHOWER, Cam paced in his living room, still only wearing the towel around his narrow hips. He hadn't shaved yet, which he'd told himself to do today, but he had more important things on his mind. Austin was late, and it made Cam annoyed as *fuck*.

Sitting down on the edge of his bed, his knee started to bounce, and he tapped the pad of his thumb along the fingertips on his right hand. Then he did the left twice. His silvery gray eyes slid to the clock above the flat screen, and he scowled.

I'm gonna punch him in the fucking face.

Cam grew impatient quickly, although he'd probably passed impatient the minute it was noon. Reaching over to the low coffee table, he snatched up his pack of smokes and a lighter, then lit one up and took a deep, calming drag. Meanwhile, he looked down and touched his thumb to the remaining four fingers on his right

7

hand. Just the tips. Over and over. While he breathed deeply through his nose.

It helped him to handle stress—something to focus on.

As had become common now, every window in the entire house—not that it was big; just a two-bedroom, one-story home—was open, and the lamps were timed to switch on at sunset. Landon, his older brother, had bought him a bunch of those timers.

Another thing that had changed was that he now slept in the living room. His bed had replaced the couch. It was more open and spacious than his bedroom down the hall.

He was lucky his family had pitched in to pay the bills—mortgage and utilities—while Cam was... elsewhere. They said renting it out would be like not believing Cam was still alive.

Tomorrow was his thirty-fourth birthday, and he dreaded having the house filled with family and coworkers. He wouldn't call them friends, 'cause he shied away from those. But there were four other guys working in his brother's garage, Cam not included, and they'd be here, too.

He'd thought about inviting Austin, but then he'd changed his mind. Austin would probably bring his wife and kid, and that meant more people crowding him. Plus, he'd already met Jade once and that was enough.

So not going down that path.

He was adamant about seeing Austin today, though, 'cause it had been too long. Austin had shut down around the same time they started giving their statements to the police, and now Cam was gonna intervene.

Checking the time again, he pushed back his dark hair that was in serious need of a cut, and he nodded to himself. *Fifteen minutes.* Austin was fifteen minutes late. That mother*fucker.*

Thankfully, as Cam stubbed out his smoke in an ashtray, the doorbell rang, and he was off the bed in a flash. He secured the towel around his hips and went to the door, nearly ripping it open.

"Don't you own a fucking watch?" he asked irritably.

Austin raised a brow over his glasses. Those were new, by the way. Cam hadn't seen them before, and he… he liked them. They kinda made Austin look all authoritative—

"Want me to leave again?" There was a dare in Austin's dry tone.

Cam glared and left the small hallway, counting on Austin to follow. Crossing the living room, he walked out the door that led to the small backyard. There was no grass; Cam hated mowing the lawn. When he'd bought this house a few years ago, he and his brother had taken a couple weekends to pave the area around the kidney-shaped pool with flat stones and build a wooden patio. The pool took up most of the space, and it brought back memories of some of the things he and Austin had talked about missing when…

Cam shook his head, not wanting to think about it. Instead he sat down in a chair and waited for Austin to join him. There was a cooler with beers between two chairs, and depending on how long Austin stayed, there were two steaks in the fridge, soaking in marinade.

There was also an umbrella to shield them from the worst of the sun.

The steaks and the beer made it worth popping an endless amount of Pepto. Yeah, his fucking nutritionist had told him to stick to "stomach-friendly" foods for now, but if he wanted a fucking steak, he'd eat one.

Austin eventually walked out and sat down, too, and he was dressed appropriately for this weather—cargo shorts and a T-shirt. It was fucking insane how much clothes had come to matter to Cam and possibly the others who had been taken, as well. 'Cause you took a lot of shit for granted. Like wearing what you wanted.

During… *that time*… Cam had been stuck in the coveralls he wore at the garage. Which he'd never wear again. Landon had already assured him he could work in other clothes—when he eventually returned to work, of course.

"Riley didn't want to leave earlier," Austin sighed, explaining why he was late. "Took a while to convince her."

Cam nodded with a dip of his chin, having heard countless stories of Austin's little girl. He'd even met Riley himself, but it had been a short moment with too many family members in a small space. Cam didn't like small spaces. Never had.

He liked them even less now.

"She doesn't look like you," he stated for no reason at all. He was still trying to simmer down from before, and maybe insignificant bullshit would help. "Just the hair." He remembered light brown hair that matched Austin's, but that was about it. Or maybe her eyes, too? Fuck it. He wasn't sure.

Austin didn't reply to that. "Are you taking your meds?"

Cam rolled his eyes and grabbed a beer. "Who are you—my fucking father? Yeah, I'm taking my meds. Christ." He was lying.

He hated his meds.

Austin sighed again.

Still feeling agitated and antsy, Cam chugged down his first beer quickly and then leaned back in his chair, reminding himself that Austin was here now. Nothing had gone wrong. It was just Riley who'd been reluctant to leave her dad.

It sucked that they lived in completely different parts of the city. On opposite sides, even.

"So… big birthday tomorrow." Austin went for conversation again.

"Not really." Cam closed his eyes and breathed calmly. "Thirty or forty would've been big. Or even thirty-five. Not thirty-four."

If anyone had a big birthday coming up, it was Austin. In December, he'd turn forty. Cam remembered that from one of the times he'd had an anxiety attack in that metal cage. Austin had calmed his ass down with useless trivia about accounting, childhood stories, and some other personal crap that had made Cam focus on something other than his hyperventilating.

After a moment, he opened his eyes and lolled his head to the side, facing Austin, who was silently watching him. With Austin around, Cam was both relaxed and distressed. There was something about Austin's presence that Cam had grown to want more of, yet there was something else that left him dissatisfied. Almost as if he'd been teased mercilessly and then been left hanging.

It irritated Cam. A lot. And he refused to delve deeper into it, 'cause he knew where it would lead.

"You have weird fucking eyes," he muttered with a frown. Depending on how the light hit Austin, they could be brown, green, and even bluish. Weird. Now they were a mix between green and gold, but then again, the umbrella was yellow. Sighing, Cam closed his eyes again and tapped the pad of his thumb to his fingertips. Index finger, middle finger, ring finger, fuckin' pinky. Repeat.

"Are you all right?" Austin asked quietly.

"Yeah. And I should be asking you that." Cam's reply was mumbled as he finally reached a higher state of calm. His breathing slowed and his eyelids felt heavier. "Have you been sleepin' any?"

"Not much," Austin admitted, and Cam could hear the exhaustion in his tone.

"The shrink gave you sleeping pills, didn't she?"

"Yep. But I don't like them."

Cam could relate. He didn't like them, either. They made him loopy, which in turn made him feel less in control of himself. Control was fucking important. Vital. It was something he'd struggled with since he was born, but he'd never been so robbed of it than during those five months in a humid, basement hell.

AUSTIN WASN'T SURE how much time had passed, but he figured he'd been at Cam's house for quite a while when he noticed that Cam had fallen asleep in the deck chair.

Much like himself, Cam suffered from nightmares and

flashbacks, so Austin thought about waking him. He studied the younger man, who had lost weight, too. They were still both fairly muscular, though Cam was a bit slighter with his narrow hips, but it was clear several pounds of fat and muscle had been lost.

Cam's pale body was decorated both intentionally and not. Along his ribcage, inked vines tangled in barbed wire and song lyrics snaked up to his shoulder. From there, countless tattoos covered his right arm. An angel from behind with black wings, a skeleton he recognized as a famous rock band's mascot, more lyrics, a vintage car, a few darkly colored puzzle pieces, names, dates, an old-fashioned microphone, a pair of drumsticks forming an "X," a snowflake, and two words that had stuck with Austin from the moment he'd spotted them. Along the old-fashioned microphone's cord that lingered down between several other tattoos, the words "wired differently" had been inked on a loop. Over and over, those two words followed the mic's cord.

The good memories from their months in that cell could probably be counted on one hand. The time Cam told Austin the stories behind his tattoos was one of them. Now, his mind voluntarily drifted there.

In the meantime, Cam had no choice. Trapped by sleep, a nightmare pulled him back to the very same cell; only, he wasn't discussing ink.

THE FUCKER, WHOMEVER he was, who had kidnapped Cam as he was getting off work three days ago, usually left the faint florescent lights on, but *there were times he left his victims in the dark, too. Right now was one of those times. Without windows, there was no sense of time and direction, but the man who'd been thrown into his cage yesterday was sleeping fitfully, so maybe it was night.*

Austin, the man had said his name was, was only wearing a pair of sweatpants with a local construction company's logo on them and a T-shirt. So, Cam idly guessed Austin worked in construction, which a couple other guys here did, too. There was also a plumber, a bus driver, a bartender, two without jobs, and one mailman. All males. All between thirty-two and forty-four years of age.

Since Cam had been locked up in here, he had spent his time fighting off anxiety attacks, shouting for help, regulating his motherfucking breathing, and learning the names of the other eight fuckers in here. He'd found out that they were all stuck in small cells two by two—Victor and Chase, Lance and James, Tim and Sean, Pete and Chris. And now Cam and Austin.

They were names he'd remember involuntarily, 'cause it was nothing he gave a flying fuck about at this point. All he cared about was the fact that ten seemingly able-bodied men had gotten themselves kidnapped. And as far as they all knew, only one man was responsible. In other words, shit didn't look good.

He'd read the papers, of course, so he knew that the first dude had been taken about a week before Cam was kidnapped, too. It was big news in the entire state, and now the number was up to ten kidnappings in less than two weeks.

Cam wished he could say he'd fought for his life when he'd been taken, but that would be a lie. After work, he'd stopped to pick up some food on his way home, and the motherfucker had blindsided him. Maybe it was chloroform; it didn't matter. Cam had dropped in a few seconds, and before that, the shock had worked against him. He'd already been immobile, making it embarrassingly easy for that son of a bitch.

He hoped his precious Camaro was okay. If anything, Landon would immediately know something was wrong, 'cause Cam would never just leave that baby behind.

The sounds of muffled mumbling and muttering from a few others were cut off abruptly when a heavy door slammed open—a noise that was now so familiar that they all knew who it was.

Each time that door opened, Cam vowed to struggle if he got the opportunity. He promised himself to fight, which wasn't easy wearing cuffs, but fuck if he was gonna surrender that easily. He had failed when Austin had been thrown in here, because the kidnapper, who hid behind a black mask, had drawn a goddamn gun on him.

"Good morning!" Psycho sounded like he'd been drinking too much whiskey during his days. "Now that I've filled every work position, I suppose it's only fair you know who your employer is."

Stunned silence blanketed the entire basement. Based on the lack of windows and how the men sometimes heard footsteps above them, they'd guessed they were being held in a basement. That was all, though.

The crazy motherfucker continued. "You will refer to me as Sir or Mr. Stone. I am your boss, and I will hand out your schedules shortly."

Across the small cage, Cam heard Austin suck in a breath.

"How about letting us outta hea', you sick son of a bitch?!" a man farther away shouted. He had a thick New York accent, and Cam hadn't heard him speak before.

"Silence!" Psycho boomed out.

THREE

CAM WAS IN purgatory when someone woke him up. Disoriented and ready to fight for his life, he flew out of his chair and pounced on the fucker touching his arm. Vision blurry, he gripped Psycho by the throat and they ended up on the floor—

"Cam!"

What the fuck?

The sound of Austin's voice made Cam slow down his movements.

"Jesus Christ, Cam," Austin growled. And with a force Cam couldn't compete against, he ended up on his back, his shoulder blades digging into the wooden boards of the patio. Shit. Patio. He was back home. Not hell. Not that metal cage. Austin was here. They were safe.

Cam released a choked breath and tried to relax under Austin's body.

Austin must have noticed. He loosened his grip on Cam but didn't move away. Now Austin wasn't holding him down to defend himself, it seemed. It was to comfort. He leaned down and cupped Cam's cheek and rested their foreheads together. It was a contact that had worked for them before.

The next time Austin spoke, it was gentler. "Talk to me, Cam. You're a mess." He brushed his thumb over the shadows under Cam's eyes.

"I'm sorry," he muttered in a strangled voice. "Fuck. I don't—" *I don't know what's wrong with me.*

Well, he had a guess, but he refused to go there. His shrink had told all of them about PTSD, and Cam didn't want to add another issue to his already-long list. PTSD was a condition that felt so permanent—the last thing he needed in his life. But it had been like this whenever someone startled him awake, so he knew he needed to address the problem.

At the hospital, it had been his brother. Then, a few days after he'd been released, he'd hooked up with one of the chicks who never stopped calling him. He had fallen asleep at her apartment after a mediocre fuck, and when she'd woken him up, she had been on the receiving end of a fist.

He'd felt beyond shitty. Savannah had been understanding— had even tried to comfort Cam while he took her to the emergency room for her split lip, and she'd offered to drive him to his shrink's office afterward. Cam had passed on the offer, apologized a hundred times, and then ended their casual relationship.

He wasn't gonna take a chance with Kim or Brian, the other

two he'd hooked up with from time to time. He'd ended things with them, too. Kim had cried, reminding Cam of how women could get—*so much for casual fucking*—and Brian had been oddly quiet.

There was also another reason Cam had already planned on never seeing Brian again, and that reason was currently lying on top of him. Being with a guy would cause Cam to think about things other than being friends with Austin, a man he needed in his life.

"Have you spoken to Gale about this?" Austin asked as he slowly removed himself from Cam. They went to the same psychologist—all the surviving guys did. "You should. It could be PTSD."

"Yeah, yeah," Cam grumbled and pulled himself up. Giving Austin a hand, he helped him up, too. "Sorry I attacked." He adjusted the towel on his hips.

"I can take it."

The two men stood before each other, close enough to touch, and maintained eye contact. It made Cam wonder if Austin found their relationship odd. 'Cause closeness was as easy as breathing to them. So was touching. Personal space was usually so fucking important to Cam, but with Austin…

Austin broke the spell, clearing his throat, and plopped down in his chair again. Then he pulled out a bottle of painkillers from a side pocket of his shorts, and Cam gave him a cocked eyebrow.

"Headache," Austin answered. "These glasses are taking some getting used to. Plus, the sun…" He shook his head and sighed. "You know how it is."

"They look good on you," Cam commented before thinking. *Fuck.* He sat his ass back down in the chair and rolled his eyes at himself. "Only thing missing is the suit, Mr. MBA."

Nice save, jackass.

"And you're a dick," Austin said, removing his glasses to rub his eyes.

"You wanna go inside instead?" Cam was already standing up. While he'd had issues adjusting to the sun, too, it wasn't as bad as the man next to him. "Come on—bet there's a game on or something. You hungry?"

"Not really, but a game sounds good." Austin followed him inside. "So, mind telling me why there's a bed in here?" He waved a hand at the living room.

"My bedroom's fucking tiny," Cam lied. His bedroom was just fine, but he still felt like he was locked in. "There's a chair over there if you prefer that. I'm just gonna get some snacks." He jerked a thumb over his shoulder in the direction of the kitchen. "You want anything other than beer? Coke, water—think there's some decaf iced tea that Jules left, too."

"Coke, thanks." Austin nodded and moved toward the entertainment center while Cam headed to the kitchen. "Jules is your sister-in-law, right?"

"Yeah." Cam opened his fridge, having not gotten over his newfound greed for choosing his own meal. Just *looking* at food felt nice. "Annoying as fuck, but you gotta love her, I guess. They're having twins in a few months." He pulled out some fixings to make a few sandwiches.

His brother Landon was pale with dark features, same gray

19

eyes as Cam, and Jules took after her Mexican mother. She was also fucking tiny, so it was a little amusing to see her walking around with a big bump on her belly. And she wasn't even close to term yet.

He'd been shocked to see the baby bump on Jules when he'd been reunited with his family after the kidnapping. He knew about the IVF trials, obviously, but not that Landon and Jules had gone through another round in... what, January? Anyway, that shock had quickly morphed into excitement for his brother and sister-in-law.

Austin hummed, then went quiet for a beat before he chuckled. "Well, your porn stash wasn't hard to find."

Cam laughed and figured Austin had taken a guess on the one cabinet in the entertainment center that came with a lock. "Wouldn't wanna freak out my mom. Dad and Landon advised me to lock it up." His father's exact words had been, *"Let's not give your mother any ideas."*

"You don't think Lily's ever seen porn?" Austin snorted.

Cam was impressed. After having only met his parents briefly at the hospital, Austin had evidently formed a fairly accurate view of Lily and Jonathan Nash. Well, at least Lily, who was very free-spirited and carefree. She'd been the Irish hippie from San Francisco who'd fallen for a more conservative architect. Not that there was anything conservative left in Cam's dad. Now he was the mellowed-out voice of reason who kept Lily grounded. And in return, Lily made sure Jonathan never forgot how to spell "fun."

Grinning to himself, Cam took the food and drinks and returned to the living room. "Not porn with dudes doing each other." He set down Coke, beer, chips, and the sandwiches. "All right. Let's see what's on." He sat on the edge of his bed and grabbed the remote. The large flat screen flickered to life; meanwhile, Austin sat down next to Cam, and he appeared to be confused.

"Dudes?"

Cam gave him a sideways glance. "Yeah." He left it at that, not wanting to elaborate, and faced the TV, quickly finding one of the sports channels. "You mind if I...?" He pointed to the smokes and the ashtray on the coffee table. All the windows and the patio door were still open, but he didn't know if Austin was okay with it.

"Go ahead." Austin shrugged.

It looked like he was somewhere else. Miles away, in fact. That worried Cam, 'cause he knew firsthand where he involuntarily ended up when his mind wandered.

"WHAT THE FUCK?" Cam scratched his scruffy chin and scowled at the paper. "It says here that I'm a deadbeat punk hiding behind a smile."

This was just a nightmare, right?

"It's not a schedule." Austin was scanning his own paper, absently spinning the wedding band on his finger. Like in old prison movies, there was a hatch in the door. That was where their kidnapper had slipped in the papers. "It's a script." In the faint fluorescent light, they saw what were obviously instructions for characters. Nothing "schedule" about it. There were traits, hobbies, and vague descriptions.

"He's gotta be certifiable." Cam looked around himself warily.

In the small cell, they were surrounded by metal. Only the back wall was different; it was drywall strengthened with metal panels. Even the dirt floor was enhanced with a metal net—to prevent digging, he supposed.

Nothing around them could be used as a weapon.

Between the unyielding cots they'd never call beds was a bucket of water, a washcloth, and a bar of soap. They each had a blanket. Next to the solid, steel door there was a chrome-like toilet attached to the wall. The toilet paper was of the cheapest industrial kind.

For utensils, they'd been given plastic spoons and a tin cup.

That was it. And now the scripts.

"Has anyone tried to overpower him?" Austin whispered.

Cam shrugged, craving a cigarette. "How? I've never even seen him. He doesn't open the doors, as far as I know. Only when someone new comes, and…" He swallowed, glared, and averted his eyes. "He aimed a gun at me when you were thrown in here. I-I froze." He chuckled without humor. "Thirty-three years old and I froze like a fuckin' kid."

Austin frowned and took in his surroundings for the umpteenth time. "What about food delivery? Change of water?"

Cam jerked his chin, gesturing to the wall they shared with the neighboring cell. "Those two guys next to us are refusing to send out or accept anything. So, Psycho doesn't bother to knock. At least that's how it's been for the past two days."

"Psycho." Austin snorted. "Fitting. And original."

Cam scowled. "You got a better name for him? 'Cause that's what we should focus on here, right? His fucking name."

Austin quieted and looked down at his papers again.

Cam did the same, and what he could conclude was that they all had *roles to play, and for the sake of keeping his sanity, he chose to see the silver lining. With a task assigned to him, it wasn't likely the kidnapper had plans to kill him, right? Yet. Or whatever.*

They needed to stall until they either found a way out or until the police tracked them down.

After several days in captivity, it became clear just how unstable their kidnapper was. Not only did he wish everyone a merry Christmas when he delivered their meals one day, but he also told them to relax and take a few days off work to be with family.

For the record, it was February.

Another thing: Mr. Stone now wanted to be called Mr. Cold.

During the "holidays," he only came down to the basement to deliver food and change the water in the buckets. Well, he did it for those who weren't on strike. Those who poured the old water from the bucket down the toilet and then held it up under the hatch so "Psycho" could stick in a garden hose and fill it up again were treated slightly better. They accepted the food and got the usual chicken soup, stale bread, and a tin cup of lukewarm milk. The bowls for the soup were made of hard paper.

THE GAME AUSTIN wasn't following had been on for almost thirty minutes when he checked the time. He had to leave within the hour if he wanted to be home for dinner, and it wasn't really an option. Riley would be upset if he broke his promise.

He wasn't ready to drive home just yet, though. His mind kept going back to Cam's casual words about his, uh, movie collection. Gay porn? Was that what he meant? Austin had never really given it any thought, but he'd figured Cam was straight. He knew there were a couple women Cam met up with now and then; he'd found out about that at the hospital.

To go even further, Austin never really thought about sexual orientation at all. His parents had raised him that way after a cousin of his on his dad's side had come out as gay and Austin's aunt and uncle hadn't reacted well. Instead, Griffin and Maggie Huntley had swooped in.

Austin's cousin, Derek, was a few years older, and he'd come out right before he took off for college on the East Coast. So, it wasn't like Derek had moved in with Austin's family, but his parents had still intervened. They'd become surrogate parents to Derek, the ones who called and asked how everything was, sent care packages to his dorm, and invited him home for all the holidays.

Maggie had said, *"They're not gay people. They're people. It's pretty darn simple."*

She had been so furious at Griffin's brother for basically shunning his own son, and who could blame her? Austin didn't understand why it was a big deal, period. But now? He couldn't help but wonder about Cam and his preferences.

The thought of Cam getting off to gay porn shot tingles of something unidentifiable through Austin.

The closest Austin had gotten was the threesome he'd drunkenly had with a girl and another guy when he was at USC. He didn't really remember a whole lot of that night, though. It was one of the rare times his roommate had managed to pull the stick out of Austin's ass and dragged him away from his studies to go out.

"The Bruins are really killing it," he heard Cam say.

"Huh?" Austin snapped back to the present. "Oh, yeah. They're good."

"Wow, you're really out there." Cam studied him, a smile on his face but concern in his eyes. "The hockey season hasn't even started yet. And unless you're secretly from Boston, I can't allow Bruins fans in my home."

Austin frowned and zeroed in on the game—which was obviously a rerun, and it was basketball. His frown morphed into a scowl, and he felt a flare of anger surging up. Jesus, he had to get a grip. At any hour of the day, he could get irrationally angry for no reason.

"This was actually one of the reasons I wanted you to come over today," Cam said and lit up a smoke. "Something's up. Do you notice that you shut down and space out?"

Austin knew, but this hadn't been one of those times. Now… Cam was worried about him, but all he'd been thinking about was whether or not Cam liked cock.

He made a face and adjusted in his seat. "I have it under control," he lied. "I have a session with Gale tomorrow. We talk… about it."

"About what?"

"About, you know." Austin's shoulder tensed up, and he got defensive, more anger spiking. "What about your own damn issues, huh?" He shook his head and stood up. "Never mind. I have to go."

Austin didn't give Cam a chance to react before he left.

He knew he was being a coward, running away like that, but he couldn't deal with it right now. In captivity, both men had tackled their problems whether they wanted to or not. It had gotten to the point where nothing intimidated them—not even weapons. They'd been desperate for freedom, for the chance of healing.

Four words had become their motto: *"Gun or no gun."* Regardless of obstacles, they'd fight for their lives. But now they were hiding. They couldn't even be truthful with each other.

FOUR

GALE, A PATIENT woman, was in her mid-forties, Austin guessed. Wavy, black hair, brown eyes, kindness ever present, and red lipstick on her teeth. She could stare all day long, never breaking the silence that stretched on. She had asked him about his anger, and he didn't want to answer. He didn't know *how* to answer.

Austin felt like a damn fool for being here.

As much as he resented Jade for asking him to forget it all and leave the past in the past, he wanted to do the same. He wanted to go back to normal where he knew what he was doing. Things were simpler then. He'd wake up, get ready, eat breakfast, take Riley to school if Jade had an early meeting, then head off to work, crunch numbers, analyze statistics, hold meetings, report to the main office in LA, come home, eat dinner, help Riley with her homework, watch some TV, go to bed, on occasion make love to his wife... On weekends, they'd spend time as a family, go visit

Riley's grandparents—do normal stuff together. There were barbecues, day trips, vacations.

Yesterday after he had left Cam's house, he'd been passive and silent while Jade prepared dinner. He'd pretended to listen to Riley's retelling of her day at the zoo with Austin's folks. Then, that night, he'd *fucked* Jade for the first time. Ever.

He had always been an attentive lover, but he didn't feel it anymore. He had so much shit bottled up inside him; there was no patience, no tenderness, no foreplay. He had fucked her, plain and simple, and Jade had moaned in all the right places, but he wasn't stupid. She hadn't liked it at all.

Austin wasn't himself anymore, and it unnerved him.

Jade certainly didn't like the new version of him.

"Things aren't easy anymore," he said, shifting in his seat. Today was the first day in months he was wearing a suit. He didn't know why he'd put it on this morning. Perhaps it was to feel more like his old self? Regardless, it wasn't working. "There's no, uh…" He searched for the right word. "Stability."

"Understandable." Gale nodded. "It will take time to get back to what you're used to—if it'll ever happen. You need to remember that what you've been through has changed many things."

Austin didn't need that reminder.

"How have you spent your days since you were released from the hospital?" Gale asked with a tilt of her head.

He sighed and leaned back, thinking mainly about Riley. "I've done what you suggested; I've spent time with my family. I've taken things slowly, readjusting and so on." He ran a hand through his light brown hair. It wasn't as styled as it had been in the past. No wax. It used to be a lot shorter than the three or so inches it was now, and it was messy, to boot. There was also a night's worth of scruff, and he hadn't bothered with cologne or anything. He didn't feel like it. "I've... relaxed?" He didn't know why that came out as a question.

"You don't like relaxing?" she guessed.

Austin shrugged. "It was easier when I had a routine to follow."

When Gale asked him what a "normal" day entailed, Austin told her—in great detail. From the breakfast he usually ate and how he got ready in the morning, to how they worked together in the evenings with dinner, homework, clearing the table, and going to bed.

"That's not only about liking routines," she said gently. "It's also about being in control. You know what's happening around you, and you know your tasks. You prefer a well-oiled machine because nothing is strange or new. And, Austin—" she leaned forward in her seat "—you weren't in control when you were held against your will. It's no wonder you're angry."

Austin said nothing, though her words did make sense. But it wasn't only about that. He felt like... like a... damn, he didn't even know. A failure? Maybe. Because in the past, he hadn't failed when it really mattered. He was a decent husband, a good father, and he could provide for his family. He made sure to take time aside with his girls, too. A weekend here with Jade, a weekend there with Riley.

Now there was no routine. There was a bunch of new crap,

and… there was Cam.

He frowned and looked down.

AUSTIN BEGAN TO notice how fidgety and agitated Cam became the crazier their kidnapper turned out to be. He was repeating things to himself, too. Over and over, Cam would mumble about loss of control as he seemed to tap his fingers together. No, Austin changed his mind; it was the pad of his thumb that he tapped to his other fingers. Cam's… quirk… caused his cuffs to clink softly with each movement, and that *annoyed Austin.*

In turn, Austin's constant pacing and need to check the bolts and screws in the walls seemed to irritate the ever-loving fuck *out of Cam.*

"You're only making it worse," Austin snapped one day, referring to Cam's wrists. They were a lot redder than Austin's, even bleeding in one spot. "Jesus Christ. Why haven't the police found us yet?" He pulled at his hair, feeling like he was going crazy. "There has to be a way out."

"Yeah. Psycho only forgot to tell us," Cam said dryly.

Austin shot him a glare.

"HE KEPT TALKING about control." Austin stared out the massive window behind Gale. "I didn't know I'm just as dependent on it." Only, Austin didn't get anxiety attacks like Cam did. He grew angry. Furious, even.

"Where are you now, Austin?" Gale asked softly. "Who are you talking about?"

Austin cleared his throat and straightened. "Cam. Back when... *back then*, Cam would talk about losing control. We weren't in control. And he had anxiety attacks." Thinking back on it only made him angrier. "He was a damn pain to help," he chuckled darkly. "I know the reason, obviously, but..." Being unable to help—that was a major trigger, he realized. And now, now he couldn't even help *himself.*

When he faced Gale again, she was studying him curiously, and Austin didn't blame her. He was mumbling nonsense, everything out of context; of course she was confused. At least, he figured she was confused. Hell, so was he.

"Austin, do you feel like Cam was or is your responsibility?"

IN ANOTHER PART of Bakersfield, Cam was in the living room opening his gift from Landon and Jules. Well, there wasn't a lot to open; it was a box with a lid, and it was moving. He grinned and flipped up the lid, then hid the fact that he felt like shedding tears of relief. Why he hadn't thought of this himself was beyond him.

He would feel safer now. Call it a gut feeling.

"If you don't like him, Landon and I have already talked about getting a dog," Jules said quickly, looking worried.

Cam squatted down and petted the head of the Husky pup. "Nah, this guy ain't going anywhere."

Landon and he had had a Husky when they were kids. A damn good dog. This one was definitely gonna keep Cam active, too. That was a good thing. Huskies weren't put on this earth to mosey around and be lazy.

"How old is he?" He picked up the puppy. He chuckled as the dog licked his face, and just like the one he'd had as a kid, this one had light blue eyes and a cream and light brown-colored coat.

"Twelve weeks." Landon smiled at the puppy and his little brother. "You're gonna have to pick out two names."

Cam nodded and ignored the other party guests in the backyard. It was calmer here in the living room. "You think Mom will be pissed if I name this one after a drink, too?"

Landon smirked. "You were seven the last time. You weren't supposed to know about booze yet."

Well, their dad had approved of Irish Coffee. Two names—a dog had to have two names; it was a rule. Irish for short.

Cam wasn't big on affection with just anyone; personal space was important, but his brother and Jules weren't strangers. They'd earned his trust years ago. Walking over to them, he kissed Jules on the cheek and hugged Landon, saying thanks more than once. He doubted they knew how much he appreciated this kind of gift.

"Thank you," he said again, averting his gaze to the puppy. When shit got emotional, he didn't like direct eye contact. "What do you think about keeping it Irish?" After all, their mother was Irish, even though she was born in Cali. Her maiden name was Mulligan. "Or we could piss off Mom and say we're keeping it Irish, then we call him Bourbon."

God forbid if Lily Nash was around to hear you call Irish whiskey bourbon, or even worse, Scotch. The woman knew her booze.

"Harsh," Jules laughed.

"How would she know your intention?" Landon countered.

Cam shrugged. "Bourbon Mulligan oughta do it." He nuzzled the soft patch of fur on the top of the puppy's head. "Yeah, I'm sticking with it. Bourbon." Hey, it went well with the dog's coloring, too. "Let's go introduce the Irish." He grinned and carried Bourbon out on the patio where his parents were talking to some of the guys from Landon's garage and a few cousins on Jonathan's side. "Mom." He came up behind her and draped an arm around her shoulders. "I want you to meet Bourbon Mulligan."

Lily stared up at her youngest son with a blank expression.

"Oh, boy." Jonathan snorted. "Here we go."

"You think that's funny?" Lily asked flatly. "You know, honey, I'm all for peace and love, but perhaps you're not too old for a damn spanking—"

"Oh!" Cam cracked up. "You kiss your husband with that mouth?" He winked and left his parents to grab a beer.

Everyone knew Cam didn't like to be crowded, so they didn't get too close when he sat down on one of the patio chairs next to Landon. He sipped his beer, mostly staying quiet, and watched as his new dog played around with a tennis ball.

It was the only toy he had in his house, so he made a mental note to pick up some more tomorrow. From the guys at work, he was given a gift card to a pet superstore, a bag of puppy food, a leash, and a bowl set for food and water, all of which had Jules's name written over them. That was how men worked. They handed their money to the women, who went shopping.

"You got the usual from Mom and Dad?" Landon asked.

Cam nodded. That meant five hundred bucks in a savings bond and a year's subscription to *Hot Rod* and *Automobile*.

Bringing out his new phone—the old one was lost the day he was kidnapped—he snapped off a shot of Bourbon and texted it to Austin with the caption, *"My new housemate."*

"Who'd you send that to?"

"Austin," Cam mumbled, eyeing the bandages on his wrists. They were coming off soon, and he knew he'd always have to live with the scars. He had scars all over his body, but these were the deepest. Five months of being cuffed almost constantly had made sure of that.

"Yeah, he was here yesterday, wasn't he?" Landon asked and grabbed a handful of peanuts from the table. "I'm surprised Ethan hasn't spoken to you about that guy."

"*Who?*" Cam's head snapped in his brother's direction.

Landon frowned, confused, and nodded at the dudes by the grill. "Ethan? Jack's partner. Said he thought it was a shame Austin was straight or whatever." He rolled his eyes. "He read about the Huntleys in the papers—saw Austin's picture."

"Right." Cam breathed in through clenched teeth, feeling stupid. He thought his brother had said *Evan*. Big difference. Jesus fucking Christ.

A WEEK OR *so later, their "boss" came down and announced his name was now Mr. Strong and that he wanted to speak to Evan.*

There was no response.

"Insane motherfucker." Cam brought both hands up to push back some of his hair.

He reeked, despite washing off daily and using that fucking bar of soap, but it didn't matter. It was humid down here and smelled of mildew. On top of that, at least one had vomited and missed the fucking toilet. It also smelled like piss, which almost made Cam wish they had an impenetrable roof to their cell, too. Alas, it was a metal cover with finger-width sized holes everywhere. Just enough for the light to seep through when Psycho decided they'd had too much darkness.

And Christ, he needed a smoke. Bad. Hell, it would make the place smell better.

"Wait. The scripts." Austin kept his voice low. "It said another name on mine." He picked up the papers off the floor and pointed to the top corner. "Sam."

"There's no Evan here!" someone shouted angrily.

Cam frowned as he spotted the name on his script, as Austin called it.

"It says Evan on mine," he whispered.

"I DON'T FUCKING get it," Landon was saying, but Cam wasn't really following. He was busy steadying his breathing. "Do they share dudes? I mean, if Jules said it was a shame some other man was gay, I would pound his ass."

"He'd probably like that," Cam replied automatically.

It earned him a punch on his arm. "That's not how I meant it, bro." Landon scowled at how easily he'd fallen into that one. "But can you answer my question?"

"What question?"

Landon took on an impatient expression. "Do gay guys generally share each other?"

Cam couldn't help but laugh. "Christ, you're stupid. Why the fuck would they?" He thought back on Jack's partner's comment about Austin. "It was probably just a compliment, idiot."

"Well, how would I know? I'm not gay."

"You say that as if I am."

"You do play for both teams," Landon pointed out.

Cam shrugged. "So fucking what? Does that make me an expert?" Sometimes his brother could be dumb. "I can't believe we're even talking about this. What are you, a fucking woman?"

Landon didn't miss a beat. "See the belly on that one?" He pointed at Jules, who was laughing about something with their mother. "I think that proves what I'm equipped with."

"Whatever." Cam sighed as his phone beeped with a text from Austin, or Mr. MBA, as he was labeled in his contact list.

If Riley sees that, she'll run away from home and we'll find her at your place. I'm deleting this photo now. Happy birthday, by the way.

Cam smiled to himself and pocketed the phone. At first he'd been a little worried Austin's abrupt departure yesterday would cause a rift or something, but apparently not. Then again, they'd fought before, and that hadn't changed anything.

LATER THAT NIGHT, when it was only Cam and Bourbon in the

house, the wounds of today's flashback were too fresh for him to relax.

All the windows remained open, screens in place to keep out the bugs, and the lights were on. But it wasn't enough. Sitting on the bed in his living room, he struggled to not think back, to not feel like he was suffocating.

"I'm not Evan," he mumbled to himself, tapping his thumb to his other fingers. "I'm not Evan." Someone else was. "I'm not Evan." The profiler at the FBI had pieced together a lot about the motherfucker who had kidnapped ten guys, but all they had was an educated guess. "I'm not Evan."

His breathing wasn't slowing down, but he hated taking a pill for his goddamn anxiety disorder. Before the kidnapping, he hadn't had an attack in so fucking long, and now they were ruling his life. But there was one thing that had worked in captivity. Or rather, someone.

He swiped up his phone and called Austin.

FIVE

RILEY HAD GONE to sleep, the dishwasher had been emptied, the house was spotless, a movie was playing, and Austin couldn't sit still. He was supposed to watch the romantic flick with his wife, but it was impossible to relax.

After his session with Gale today, he had called his boss at the main office in LA, and he'd been told not to come back yet. Take another month off, Mr. Sterling had advised, though it was more of an order. Another month. A whole *fucking* month—with nothing to do.

"Christ, you're all twitchy!" Jade exclaimed in frustration. "*Please*, just... just calm *down*." She was pleading with him now. "You promised you'd leave all that behind you."

Austin's jaw ticked with tension and he nodded, then faced the TV again and adjusted his glasses. Not that he watched. Now he had to physically make sure he didn't move a muscle.

He needed *something* to do. As much as he adored spending time with his daughter now that she was on summer break, he needed more than that. Something that was just for him. He was even sick of seeing his parents constantly popping in to say hello. God knew he loved them, but it was becoming frustrating to see his mother in tears. All the what-ifs were getting tedious.

Gale was right; he did need to take it slow, and he knew if he was running the show all on his own, he would soon be buried in work. Then, one day, he'd probably explode. But walking around doing absolutely nothing wasn't good, either. Yes, it gave him time to process and heal, but it was also giving him more grays.

"You're doing it again," Jade snapped. "My God, just forget it." She shot up and shut off the TV. "I'm going to bed. Feel free to join me when you can act like a normal person."

Austin sighed heavily, his head lolling against the back of the sofa, and closed his eyes. Maybe he needed a release, he thought wryly. He could get his laptop and stream some porn, because unlike Cam, he sure as hell didn't have a DVD collection.

Porn. Relax.

He groaned and scrubbed a hand over his face. The other hand slid down his gray sweats to grip his cock.

His mind went to the hard fuck he'd given Jade last night, how damn good that had felt physically, and he pondered if that was something he needed in his life—a physical outlet. Something that exhausted his body.

He gave his half-hard cock a slow but firm stroke.

And just as unbidden thoughts about Cam entered his mind, his phone rang.

Damn it all to hell.

Dragging his body off the couch, he adjusted himself and headed to the hallway where his phone was charging next to the pile of unopened mail. The caller ID said *Cameron Nash.*

Austin grinned and checked the time before answering. "You're still the birthday boy for another hour. Thought you'd be out partying."

Cam wasn't amused. *"Do—do you have a m-minute?"*

"What's wrong?" Austin was quick to wipe away any trace of humor. Worry spiked inside him, reminding him of Gale's question about whether or not he felt responsible for Cam. He'd never answered, because he didn't know. "Are you having an anxiety attack?" For the past couple weeks, he had started reading articles and online journals about Asperger's on the internet, anything to understand more about Cam's disorder. It had freaked Austin out a bit in that metal cage, and he didn't want to feel that way ever again. *Control.* "Tell me you've taken your pill." He knew Cam had medication for his anxiety disorder, but he also knew the guy hated to take them.

"Fuck that," Cam growled, breathing heavily. *"Just talk to me. Tell me some shit about taxes or whatever."*

Austin eyed the car keys in the bowl Riley had made out of clay when she was younger. "Take your fucking pill, or I'm coming over."

"That's better." Cam forced a laugh. *"You get me all distracted when you drop the f-bomb, Mr. MBA."*

"Cameron," Austin warned and snatched up the keys to his black Mercedes. Next to the little bowl was a notepad, so he scribbled a quick note to Jade in case she'd wake up and wonder where he was. He wasn't dressed to go out, but he didn't care. Gray sweats, a black T-shirt, and his blue All Stars would have to do. Grabbing his wallet, too, he unlocked the door and snuck out.

"That's just wrong," Cam groaned. *"You don't ever use my full name. But at least it's better than Evan."*

Austin cursed as he got into his car. He guessed Cam was having flashbacks because he'd mentioned that name. While Austin hated to think back on those months as much as any of the other guys did, at least he didn't panic. Cam did.

"Did something happen today?" Austin held his phone between his shoulder and cheek as he backed out of the driveway and waited for the Bluetooth to kick in. "Flashbacks?"

"One," Cam muttered, and something crackled softly in the background, as if he was lighting up a cigarette. *"No one noticed, though. I-I managed to c-calm down."*

But he wasn't calm now. Austin could hear his rapid breathing over the phone, and it wouldn't be easy to help Cam if the name Evan was involved. It was one of the worst experiences during their time in that basement, and it had only been the beginning.

"HOW CAN YOU not react?" Austin whispered, agitated. He watched as Cam stood up, no emotions on his face whatsoever, walked the few steps to the heavy door, and announced his fake name. Evan.

Whereas Austin had spent his days looking for a way out, thinking about an escape, and checking and double checking everything in their cell,

Cam had sat on his cot. Doing nothing.

Cam didn't answer his question, instead asking one of his own. "Can you fight?"

Austin's eyebrows shot up. "I can hold my own." When he wasn't drugged, he amended internally. Drugged and cuffed. "Why do you ask?"

"It'd be fucking stupid to let this opportunity get away, wouldn't it?" Cam fired back with a cocked brow. "We gotta try to beat him."

That had Austin's immediate approval. He nodded once and stepped closer to the door, then waited as the man outside padded closer to their cell.

Soon enough, the hatch was opened, and Cam and Austin came face-to-face with the same black mask and dark brown eyes they'd seen every time food was delivered. A creepy smile slid into place as Mr. Whoever-the-hell tossed two small keys inside the cell.

"Uncuff yourselves."

Confused and on edge, Cam and Austin obeyed, not about to let this opportunity get away, either. Free hands meant leverage, for Christ's sake. There were two of them; crazy kidnapper was only one. Done deal, right?

Or not.

Once they were free of their restraints, the man on the outside said, "Now you cuff each other again. Behind your backs."

Austin gritted his teeth together, refusing to let his deflating hope show on his face. "And if we don't?"

The man smirked and raised a gun. "I shoot."

AUSTIN SHOOK HIS head, focusing on the road and Cam telling him about his new dog. It seemed to work, though not enough.

Cam's breaths still came out choppy, and he stuttered here and there. If it went on like this for much longer, he'd get dizzy from hyperventilation.

When Cam got quiet, Austin asked, "What else is new? How are Jules and the babies?" Jules's pregnancy was big news in the Nash family.

"Fuck," Cam spat out. *"I hate this shit, Austin. I f-feel like a fucking idiot."*

"Get over it!" Austin snapped. "Look, I know this isn't really you. Okay? You've already told me you haven't had regular attacks in years before this, but come on, man. What we've been through…" Obviously it was going to leave its marks. "Keep talking."

Having broken all the speed limits across town, Austin soon drove on to Cam's quiet street.

Right now, Austin didn't feel the same kind of anger he was getting used to struggling with these days. He was frustrated with his friend, but it was different. Austin didn't have to hide anything around Cam. They understood each other. They were even alike in some ways, mostly when it came to downplaying their issues.

"There's nothing else to tell, asshole!" Okay, so Cam was getting pissed. Austin could deal with that, though. Wouldn't be the first time. *"My parents were here, my b-brother and sister-in-law, couple c-cousins, a few guys from work and their women, partners, what-the-fuck-ever, and we ate, and I stuck to m-myself, and then they left, and that's it! Jesus Christ!"*

At that point, Austin rang the doorbell.

It was quiet for a beat before Cam groaned into the phone. *"Don't fucking tell me…"* Another silence, and then the door was ripped open. Cam scowled. "I thought I heard you were in a car, but I—What're you doing here?"

Austin ended the call and pocketed his phone. A stab of envy hit his chest at the sight of Cam's defined abs, but he told himself it was *just* envy—not attraction.

"I wanted to check in on you. Make sure you were okay." He lifted a brow, taking in Cam's disheveled state. He was only wearing a pair of black basketball shorts, and it looked like he'd been to hell and back. Which he had. His hair was in complete disarray, he was ghostly pale, and he had dark shadows under his eyes. "*Are* you?"

That seemed to hit a nerve. "You can stop being a goddamn mother," Cam replied with a glare as a puppy appeared at his feet. Oh yeah, Riley would go nuts over that little thing. "I know I'm not n-normal, but I'm not fucking stupid."

Austin merely smirked, though it wasn't cocky or self-assured. It was wry and small.

"Define normal," he countered quietly, meeting Cam in the doorway. "And for not being normal, you're the only person in the world who makes sense right now. What does that say about me?" That said, he passed Cam and entered the house. He half-regretted admitting those words, but they were still true.

"It tells me you should be shipped off to the funny farm," Cam said behind him, but his voice had lost all its hostility. When they reached the living room, he asked, "Dude, are you free-ballin' under there?" He jerked his chin at Austin's sweatpants.

"Why are your eyes anywhere near to notice?" Austin fired back and sat down on the bed. "So, this is the little guy." He reached down to pet Bourbon, who hadn't been trained to guard yet. He seemed to love any sign of life, and he soaked up the attention Austin gave him. "He can't be very old, can he?"

"Twelve weeks." Cam sat down next to him. "Can't believe you actually drove all the way over."

"I can leave," Austin chuckled.

Cam shook his head no, keeping his eyes on Bourbon.

FOR ABOUT HALF an hour, Cam tried to distract Austin with trivial bullshit, but then he gave up. They didn't only see Gale Peters one-on-one; they saw her in group therapy, too—Cam and the other six who had survived. And he knew Austin wanted him to get all this out. It was one of Gale's most repeated words of advice: *"Tell someone what you're feeling—someone who will listen and just let you talk."*

"Come on, Cam," Austin groaned and fell back against the bed. His feet still touched the light hardwood floor, but he was lying down, one of Cam's pillows under his head. "Take your time—I'm here for you, but get started. Gun or no gun, remember?"

Well, Cam needed a strong drink for this shit. Standing up, he padded over to the entertainment center and opened one of the cabinets that held his small stash of booze. "Drink?" He took a few glasses and a bottle of vodka for himself. He had to buy more soon; it was barely half-full.

"Bourbon if you have it—and no dog jokes."

Cam smirked to himself and grabbed a bottle of Jim Beam. "Ice?" He started toward the kitchen.

"No, thank you."

In the kitchen, he emptied an ice tray into a bowl, snatched up a bag of peanuts, then returned to the living room. Austin got his glass of bourbon, and Cam downed one shot of vodka before pouring another. In the meantime, Austin held his glass on his stomach, only lifting his head every now and then to take slow sips.

"Okay. Talk to me."

"Fuck, you don't waste time." Cam made a face and threw back the second shot. Next he poured a bigger glass and topped it off with ice. Why didn't he just keep the booze in the freezer like normal people? "I don't even know what I'm supposed to say."

He just hated remembering it all.

CAM SWALLOWED THEN exhaled shakily as he was led past wooden beams toward a narrow staircase in the basement.

Psycho had checked his cuffs already, making sure they were on tight behind Cam's back. Austin had been the recipient of a gun aimed at him, and Cam had been promised that his cellmate would get a bullet if either tried anything.

It was Austin's pointed look that left Cam confused. The two men didn't know each other for shit, but Cam had the distinct feeling that Austin wanted him to overpower Psycho anyway, regardless of threats.

With a gun pressed to his lower spine, Cam climbed the concrete steps *leading to the ground floor, his mind spinning so fast it almost left him dizzy.*

"Stop right there," Psycho said when Cam reached the top step. *Keeping the barrel of the gun pressed into Cam's body, he walked around him and unlocked the heavy, reinforced-steel door.* "No funny business." *He aimed at Cam's head this time.*

"Or you'll shoot Austin, I know," *Cam replied quietly, glaring at the motherfucker who was now walking backward. As long as he didn't take his eyes off Cam, it was gonna be hard to surprise him.*

This was the first time Cam saw the man in his entirety, not counting the black mask hiding most of his face. What he did see was blond, graying hair, black clothes, thin lips, and a body that probably hadn't seen the inside of a gym in decades. He was short, half a foot shorter than Cam's six one, and he had a beer gut that rivaled the exercise ball his sister-in-law used when she did yoga or Pilates or whatever it was.

So, this was the fucker who'd succeeded in kidnapping ten grown men.

"Or you." *Psycho shrugged with a smile.*

Awesome.

They ended up in a tiny vestibule with cement-covered walls where there were three doors, all with keypads instead of regular locks. It was a bad cover-up of what was behind the cement. Perhaps more drywall, or maybe wood. Who knew? It looked like Psycho had just slopped it up on the wall with a careless hand, leaving the surfaces uneven.

But still solid.

It sent a wave of hopelessness through Cam, 'cause not only would it be close to impossible to figure out the passwords to those keypads, but Psycho had obviously put in a lot of time to make it impossible to escape, and they didn't even know which one of the three doors led to freedom.

He was about to find out that the middle door led to purgatory.

"BREATHE, CAM." AUSTIN was murmuring to him, sitting up again, and he was rubbing Cam's back in comfort. "Focus on your breathing."

"Did—did you—" Cam gulped and clenched his teeth. "Did you want me to try—back when—" Fucking hell, he couldn't go on. He was too tense. Releasing a shuddering breath, he tried anyway. "You gave me a look right before Psycho t-took me upstairs."

He noticed it was easier when he focused on Austin instead, not his breathing. It felt good—the hand slowly stroking the exposed skin of his back.

"Did that mean you wanted me to go for it even though he'd threatened to k-kill you?"

Austin was quiet for at least a whole minute—thinking back, Cam guessed—and he was thankful Austin didn't stop touching him. It was fucking insane how soothing it was.

It was also oddly sensual, though he was willing to bet that wasn't intentional.

Cam was gonna have to be even more careful. He trusted Austin unequivocally, felt safe with him, and was undoubtedly attracted to him. Combined with the history they shared, the attachment Cam felt was powerful.

"At the time, probably," Austin admitted eventually. "I expected you to do whatever you could to save yourself."

"Shitty fuckin' answer," Cam grunted. "I'm not that selfish."

"I know. Come on, buddy." Austin gently pushed Cam back

against the bed. Alcohol forgotten. "Keep going. You lived through the next part; you can talk about it, too."

THE SMALL ROOM *was so different from everything in the basement. This reminded Cam of a cabin. The walls consisted of thick, wooden boards, and they looked like they'd been around for at least a goddamn century. He guessed there had been a window once, too, judging by the wall across the room that had an area covered with newer-looking boards, and even more patches of cement.*

It would take hours to break free.

"Sit down," Psycho grunted.

Cam eyed the small wooden table in the middle of the room. Two chairs. In a corner, there was a metal cabinet. In another, there was a hook in the ceiling and chains hanging from it.

"I don't have all day." Psycho pressed the gun to Cam's back, sending him forward. "Let's get this over with, cousin."

Cam looked at him strangely. Cousin? *What the fuck was wrong with this dude?*

"I said sit down, Evan!" Psycho shouted, suddenly furious.

When there was a gun aimed at his head, Cam gritted his teeth and walked over to the table and slumped down in one of the chairs. The room was hot, even hotter than the basement, and he cursed the fucking coveralls he was in. The top had been pushed down when he'd gotten here initially, and the arms of the durable fabric were now tied around his waist, leaving only a smudgy white T-shirt on his upper body, but his legs? Fucking hell, it was like no air reached him under the uniform.

"Okay, let's talk about how you've contributed to ruining my life," Psycho said, coming up behind Cam. *And without another word, he pistol-whipped Cam in the back of his head.*

SIX

AUSTIN KNEW BETTER than to turn off the lights in the living room; Cam had made it perfectly clear that the lights were important. But he did get up to quickly adjust the spotlights overhead, dimming the brightness so it was less likely he would get a headache from them. Then he returned to the bed and listened as Cam told him how the kidnapper had beaten him senseless.

In the meantime, Austin did whatever he could to make Cam comfortable. By now, they were both on the bed, completely sprawled out along the length of the queen-sized mattress, and Cam was using Austin's arm as a pillow.

"He k-kept shouting how I had ruined his l-life," Cam muttered with his eyes closed. "I tried to resist, but I couldn't f-fucking move."

Austin squeezed his eyes shut, remembering how he'd waited

for Cam to be returned to their cell.

"COME ON." AUSTIN'S knee bounced. His eyes were fixed on the door. "Come on, Cam."

It had to have been hours later Austin heard the door to the basement open again. What followed was the sound of someone falling down the stairs, which alarmed him. Clenching his fists behind his back, he flinched when the metal of the cuffs dug into his wrists, but he was too furious to give a rat's ass. All he wanted was one round with that madman, and then they'd see who was boss.

The door to their cage soon opened, and Austin found himself staring at Cam's lifeless body on the floor just outside the cell. If it wasn't for the shallow, rapid breaths he heard, he'd think Cam was dead.

Austin's spine turned to ice.

"Take him," Mr. Whoever-the-hell spat out, pointing his gun at Austin. In his free hand, there was what looked like a medical kit. "Take him and clean him up. I have no further use for him. Yet."

"A bit hard to help him if I can't use my hands," Austin bit out, sneering.

"Beat him!" someone down the hall screamed. Victor. "Beat him and take his keys!"

Austin barely refrained from rolling his eyes. As desperate as he was for an escape, he wasn't stupid. There was no way he could defeat a man while cuffed behind his back, not to mention the madman had a gun.

Their kidnapper only chuckled. "I suggest you get creative, then."

There was no finesse or gentleness about it. Austin was forced to drag

Cam back into the cell by his feet, and he nearly dislocated his shoulder in the process. It took time, and he couldn't imagine the pain Cam was in.

The lamp in the ceiling above their cell didn't provide much light, but Austin could still make out darkening bruises, bloody cuts, and swelling on Cam's battered body.

The door was closed behind them, and the hatch slid open next. "Uncuff yourself then him." The madman tossed the two keys on the floor, and Austin squatted down to pick them up. "Put the cuffs on again in front of you. Evan can be free of his while he sleeps the day off."

Austin dropped his cuffs on the cot next to him, then stood up and glared at the man on the outside. "Why should I put them on again?"

"I'd think Evan would want sustenance soon. Wouldn't you?"

"Fuck," Cam rasped in a whisper from the floor, "f-fuck you."

"Very well." The psychotic creep nodded. "No food or water for either of you until you're both cuffed." That said, he threw in the medical kit, shut the hatch, and left the basement.

AUSTIN RELEASED A breath and let his eyes travel down Cam's body. The scars and the tattoos made him unique. The muscles that were slowly rebuilding made him look strong. Good food made him look healthier. But he was still vulnerable, no matter how Cam hated to admit that.

Austin was unable to deny that he actually found Cam beautiful.

Perfect with all his imperfections.

As Cam sleepily mumbled about "Psycho" throwing him

around in that torture room, he turned onto his side, his front facing Austin, and Austin brushed his fingers over Cam's right wrist that was now wedged between them.

He hoped the scars from the handcuffs wouldn't be too deep, but he had a feeling that was a pipe dream. Austin was getting rid of his bandages the day after tomorrow, but Cam had another few days to go.

In captivity, they had patched each other up as best they could. They'd been each other's nurse, doctor, shoulder to cry on, and punching bag. Because it'd be a lie to say Austin and Cam got along from the beginning. They still butted heads, especially with Austin's newfound anger and Cam's short fuse, but they made it work somehow.

Austin hoped they'd be able to patch up each other's emotional wounds, too, even if it was going to take years.

AUSTIN SAT DOWN next to him on the cot, worried as hell that Cam would have a full-blown panic attack. Slowly, he pulled off Cam's shirt to inspect the damage. Jesus Christ. *Oh, there was damage, all right. There were also countless tattoos.*

"Lie down," he murmured, gently pushing Cam back. The younger man obeyed silently, his breathing still irregular, and his eyes wide open. "Can you tell me where it hurts the most?"

He rummaged through the medical kit, locating some antiseptic cream and a couple sterile pads.

When Cam failed to answer and began hyperventilating, Austin scooted closer and automatically cupped the other man's cheek, but the gesture felt too intimate. It was something he'd do to comfort his wife or baby girl, not a grown man.

As he moved his hand to Cam's shoulder instead, he started to speak quietly, words of no importance, but hopefully they'd be enough to distract Cam from whatever hell he was suffering internally.

At the same time, he cautiously ran the washcloth over Cam's wounds. Luckily, the water in their bucket was still relatively clean, and Austin wanted to get rid of as much blood as possible before starting with the pads and the cream.

He'd already scooped out two tin cups of water for later use; he figured Cam would need to drink soon. They both would, trapped in this humid hell, but Austin could probably go without for longer than Cam could.

He continued to speak about trivial things as he cleaned Cam's upper body. He absently spoke about his daughter when he noticed the violent wince Cam gave away the second Austin came in contact with his ribs, and he murmured a low curse. Was anything broken? Because they were shit out of luck in that case. There was nothing Austin could do if there was a fracture. Antiseptic cream, pads, bandages, and a small suture kit would only help with superficial wounds.

Truth be told, Austin didn't know for whose benefit he kept talking. Maybe it was for himself—to keep memories and his own identity alive and real—and perhaps it was to give Cam something else to focus on. Regardless, when he registered a slight change in Cam's posture and his breathing, the reason didn't matter. Cam was starting to relax; that was important.

By the time Austin had done his best to wipe away blood and sweat, the water in the bucket was tinted dark pink in the florescent light from above them.

"Who the fuck," Cam coughed, "names their d-daughter Riley?"

So, that's what he's found to focus on, *Austin thought wryly.* *"Glad to hear you're still the polite ol' you," he drawled with a shake of his head. "And I named my baby girl."*

After his little brother who had died of leukemia as a child.

"I didn't say it was ugly, did I?" Cam got defensive. "Just, you know…" *He shrugged, which hurt. "It's a boy's name."*

"I like you better when you're hyperventilating and can't talk," Austin snapped. "What the hell is wrong with you, anyway?" He swiped a sterile pad with antiseptic cream over Cam's jaw, and it ticked with tension. "Do you have a breathing problem or something? Oh, and what *is* up *with the damn finger tapping?" He shook his head again, annoyed, and tried to refocus on cleaning the cuts. He also made a mental note to apply some antiseptic to their wrists. Might as well enjoy their uncuffed freedom while it lasted.*

"None of your fuckin' business," Cam gritted out.

IT HAD BECOME Austin's business soon enough. Cam had told him, and because Austin hated being helpless, he now researched Cam's disorders in his spare time, which he had plenty of.

"It's too late for you to drive home now," Cam said tiredly, not opening his eyes. "You got plans tomorrow?"

Austin stifled a yawn and fished out his phone to set the alarm. If he was home before Jade left for work, there shouldn't be any problems. "Not really. I have Riley, and when Jade gets home from work, I have an appointment with Angelo." He was their physical therapist and had his own practice near the hospital.

"What does your wife do?"

Austin reached behind him to put his phone and glasses on the coffee table. "She's a medical social worker. She assesses whether or not a patient needs help after leaving the hospital." He rolled over to face Cam again and automatically draped an arm around his middle. "God, I'm exhausted." While he snatched a pillow for them to use, Cam blindly searched for something behind him and found a soft blanket to pull over them. "This is a whole lot better than the floor."

"What do you mean—oh. Right."

Yeah, the last time they'd slept this close together, it hadn't been nearly as comfortable.

"Don't fucking remind me." Cam scooted closer so their foreheads touched on the pillow. "Night."

Cam fell asleep first, and Austin found himself gazing at the man he was beginning to see in a new light. Or maybe it wasn't very new at all. The way they often hovered near each other couldn't possibly be because of simple friendship. You *wanted* to be with a friend, but that didn't explain Austin's *need* for always taking that extra step to be within reach. One of them always made that little move that brought them closer.

WHEN AUSTIN ROUSED a couple hours later, his alarm hadn't gone off yet. He was drowsy, only half-awake, and he wondered idly why he'd woken.

It wasn't Bourbon. That little thing was sleeping in a corner on what looked like a couch cushion. But Austin got his answer as soon as he felt Cam in front of him. Having shifted during the night, he was now spooning Cam, and Austin bit back a groan when he felt his morning wood pressing against Cam's ass.

Cam was deeply asleep, but he wasn't still. Austin guessed he'd been woken up by Cam pushing his body more firmly to his, and now Austin was beyond conflicted. At the same time, he was half-asleep. Not a good mix… depending on how you looked at it.

Asleep enough to remain where he was. Asleep enough to take physical pleasure from the position they were in.

Awake enough to wonder if it was just comfort, or if he really was attracted. Awake enough to know he shouldn't be here.

Asleep enough to not give a shit.

He let sleep get him again, but an ounce of consciousness lingered. Wading through blurry dreams and the knowledge of having Cam's body against him, he shifted forward just an inch or so as he slid his hand up Cam's chest. There was a slight dusting of dark chest hair, lighter than Austin's. What drew him in the most was the faint scent of detergent and Cam's aftershave. It was warm, but comfortably so, and the last thing he wanted to do was leave.

CAM BEGAN TO wake up when he sensed Austin. He froze for a split second, ready to pounce, but since he'd already acknowledged it was Austin, someone he trusted with his life, it was easy to relax again.

He wasn't completely relaxed, though. His cock had noticed how Austin's hard body was pressing against Cam's back, and he cursed under his breath. He wished he could blame this on Austin, but considering how Cam was pressing back just as much, he couldn't.

Fucking hell. This wasn't the time for this shit. He was thirty-four years old; did he really need to remind himself not to react like a teenager? Austin was not only married, but he was straight. These days, he was also Cam's closest friend.

"Christ, Austin," Cam bitched in a voice thick with sleep. "If you don't wake up and join the living, I'm gonna break one of my rules." He never brought a conquest home. His house was a sanctuary, not a place for hookups and reminders of drunken mistakes. "You won't like it, trust me. Back off." He didn't bottom for just anybody.

"What…" Austin mumbled, not yet awake.

Irritated and turned on, Cam pushed back against Austin's impressive morning wood and grumbled, "*That*. Get it away from me."

He would've moved away himself if it wasn't for the fact that he was already crammed up against the waist-high wall that was used as a partition between the seating area and the patio door. Austin Huntley was evidently a bed-hog.

Austin hummed sleepily and gave a slow thrust of his hips, the thin layers of cotton between them betraying just how hard he was against Cam's ass.

"Jesus Christ," Cam murmured, a bit out of breath. Arousal flared up, but he needed to get over that quickly. Which wasn't easy when he felt warm lips pressing a kiss to his neck. "Wake the fuck up, man."

Thank God Austin's alarm went off a couple seconds later.

Cam knew exactly when Austin woke up fully, 'cause he went completely rigid. Then he moved away and cursed, leaving Cam wondering if Austin had known they were both awake.

"Sorry." Okay, Austin knew.

"No worries." Cam looked over his shoulder to see Austin adjusting his dick in his sweats. Squinting, he was fairly positive Austin's cheeks looked a little flushed, but he couldn't be sure. Sleep and scruff were in the way. "I'm usually in your position though, so this was new." Not completely new, but whatever.

At that, Austin turned and faced him, confusion written across his features. "What?"

Cam waved it off. "Never mind. You gonna head out right now or do you wanna take a shower first?" He scratched his jaw. "There're leftovers from yesterday, but that's about it." Fuck, he really needed to get out today. Lots of shit he had to buy.

"Um." Austin rubbed his shoulder, then stretched his arms over his head. "Damn, I'm getting old." The stretching caused his T-shirt to ride up, exposing his toned stomach and the trail of hair that led down to—*goddammit*. Cam rolled his eyes at his own reaction and pulled the blanket over his head. This was why he'd banished all thoughts about Austin in the past. "I don't fucking know. Probably best I head home."

"I think I'm a bad influence on you, Mr. MBA." Cam spoke into his pillow as he willed his dick to stand down. "Even in that basement, you used proper language." Mostly, anyway. Damn and shit were one thing, but the man never said fuck. Now, though? *Fuck.*

Cam honestly only had one memory of appreciating the view when they were in hell.

CAM AND AUSTIN surrendered after a day and a half. They put on their cuffs and returned the keys and the medical kit to Psycho. Defeat hurt their egos, but they were too thirsty and hungry to wallow in it.

Once they'd devoured their food and chugged down half the bucket of fresh water, they made a pact. Strength—they needed it. They had to remain both mentally strong as well as physically. 'Cause if the authorities never found them… they'd have to rely solely on each other. Fuck, they already were.

Since Cam's bruised ribs hurt like a son of a bitch, there wasn't much he did at first, but Austin began to spend his hours of nothingness working out.

Getting rid of his filthy T-shirt, he dropped to the floor and did push-ups. Supporting himself on his knuckles, Cam noticed, which stunned him just a bit. For some reason, Austin came off as a wholesome family man. But when he worked out, he looked like nothing that would be described as wholesome.

The muscles in his back rippled with each shove off the ground, his skin glistening with sweat. His biceps bulged, his neck strained, his breathing was harsh, and he didn't fucking stop. The first pause came when Cam had counted forty push-ups, and it only lasted for ten minutes or so. Then Austin started all over again, but with crunches. Maybe his abs weren't as defined as Cam's were, but the man was still buff and strong. Broad shouldered. He was also a few inches taller than Cam.

He was fucking hot.

"Don't forget to drink," he muttered, tearing his gaze away from Austin on the floor. He was irritated for some reason. Frustrated and tense. He wanted to work out, too, but his ribs were fucking killing him.

Not for the first time since they'd been taken, Cam could kill for a goddamn smoke.

SHAKING THAT OFF before worse memories could come to mind, Cam moved over to the edge of the bed and reached for his cigarettes. A glass of watered down vodka on the table reminded him of last night and how Austin had calmed him down.

"Bourbon pissed on the floor," Austin noted.

Cam shrugged and lit up a smoke. "Piss happens."

Perhaps he could install a doggy door to the fenced backyard; he would just need to replace the whole fucking patio door, seeing as it was glass. But he wanted Bourbon to be able to run in and out whenever he wanted.

"C'mere, buddy." He leaned down and ruffled the soft fur of the pup. "I think we should go for a run before those fuckin' errands." Cam did *not* look forward to this day. He hated being around too many people.

"What're you gonna do today?" Austin sat down on the coffee table and started lacing up his shoes.

"Grocery shopping, get my cars from the garage..." Landon had taken care of Cam's two beauties—one black Dodge Demon 340 from '71, and one indigo blue Chevrolet Camaro SS from '69—while he had been away. "Need to call Gale... Thought I'd drive over to the cemetery, too." He frowned, thinking about the guys they'd lost. Unlike Austin, Cam hadn't been to the memorial, 'cause he couldn't handle that shit.

A FEW DAYS later, Mr. Stone—yeah, the motherfucker was back to that name now—tossed a disposable razor in each cell as he delivered breakfast. He also announced that he had a meeting planned with "Thomas" later that afternoon. Then he left, leaving the men tense and wary.

As Cam and Austin took turns shaving off their growing beards, several other guys began talking about their so-called schedules, and a man named Chris revealed that it said Thomas on his.

"You never told me what he did to you," Austin said quietly, watching as Cam shaved his jaw.

"Isn't it obvious?" Cam retorted bitterly. "He beat the shit outta me, and there was nothing I could do about it."

"He didn't say anything at all? Nothing to explain his, uh, behavior?"

Cam blew out a breath and ran a washcloth over his freshly shaved face. It would itch without any kind of shaving cream or aftershave, but they couldn't exactly afford to be picky. "He called me his cousin. Evan—it's his cousin, I guess. He said I'd contributed to ruining his life."

"What the fuck?!" the guy with a New York accent shouted. Cam was fairly sure by now the dude's name was Lance. "Yo, I need some help in hea'!"

"I'll be right there!" another man yelled sarcastically.

It was quiet for a while, aside from someone shuffling around in his cell.

"Christ, James." That was Lance again. *"I can't—I can't fucking stop it. I can't stop the bleeding."*

JAMES HAD ONLY been the first guy to leave in a body bag. He had taken out the sharp razor blades from the plastic handle and dragged them along the insides of his forearms and then swallowed the blades.

"Do you want me to go with you?" Austin's question brought Cam back to the present.

Cam shook his head no and swallowed hard. He needed to get rid of Austin before he embarrassed himself some more. Last night had been more than enough. "Look, I'm gonna get ready—"

"Yeah, no, of course." Austin stood up. "We'll talk later?"

"Sure thing."

When they were standing by the door, they said goodbye and Austin walked toward his Mercedes. "Wait—just one thing," Austin said, opening the door to his car. He tapped the top as if he was hesitant to speak. "Did you say something earlier about, uh, about a rule you'd break?"

Cam blinked slowly as he tried to catch up with Austin's thoughts. It hit him, and he bit back a laugh. Leaning against the doorframe, he folded his arms across his chest, feeling a smirk tug at the corners of his mouth.

"You really wanna bring that up, buddy?" He reached up and scratched his neck. This was fun. No, fuck that. This was fucking hilarious. Austin was uncomfortable, and he wasn't even looking

Cam in the eye. Eye contact was usually Cam's problem. "Maybe it's best you run on home to the wifey. All right?"

"Or maybe you should answer my fucking question, Cam," Austin snapped irritably.

"Oh-ho!" Cam laughed. Christ, he wished he could read Austin's mind right now. Closing the door behind himself, he walked down the two steps and approached. "What do you *really* wanna know?" Standing on the other side of the open car door, Cam flashed a wicked grin.

"I want to know what you meant," Austin replied imploringly. "Same goes for what you said about the position you're usually in."

This was getting good. Almost too good. "It means I'm usually on top, Austin." Cam rested his forearms on the door. "And the rule?" He chuckled. "I was just fucking with you. Give it a rest."

Austin arched a brow behind his glasses. His confidence was back. "And who are you usually on top of?"

"What the fuck, man?" Cam cracked up again, took a step backward, and widened his arms. "Are you seriously asking me that? What do you want from me, huh?"

"An answer."

Cam was starting to wonder if he'd missed something. What had been on Austin's mind lately? 'Cause this was new. "I'm usually on top of whoever I'm banging—that what you wanted to hear?" He decided to lay it all out there. "Men, women, whatever. There. You got your answer." With a shake of his head, he turned around and walked inside.

He didn't give a shit what people thought about his sexuality—*usually*. He couldn't imagine Austin having any issues, but if he did? Fuck, Cam *would* care.

Son of a bitch, this wasn't gonna be a good day. He could feel it.

SEVEN

"COME ON, HUNTLEY!" Maybe Angelo looked like a Brazilian underwear model, but he was the *devil*. "Give me ten more!" He grabbed on to Austin's knees. "Come on!"

"Fuck you," Austin grunted and did another sit-up. His T-shirt and shorts were soaked in sweat, and it had only been half an hour. It was fucking embarrassing. When he got home, maybe he'd even go into Jade's secret ice cream stash at the back of the freezer.

"Not while you're my client." Angelo winked.

Austin collapsed down on the floor and stared up at Angelo with wide eyes.

Seriously?

Perhaps there was a damn sign on Austin's forehead that read, *"I may or may not have thought about a cock today that wasn't my own."*

"Jesus," he panted, sweat burning in his eyes. He grabbed the towel near his head and wiped it down his face. "I think I'm done." And not just for today.

Austin was a damn mess, inside and out. His body was aching from the brief workout, and his mind... there were no words. Instead of thinking about what Cam had said this morning, he was just pissed. He grew angry for nothing. Angry for not being able to do twenty-five sit-ups without gasping for air, angry for his physical reaction to Cam earlier, angry at Jade for not understanding him, angry at himself for the same reason, angry at his boss for telling him not to come back yet, and angry for... basically everything and everyone—not counting his daughter.

That was probably the only aspect of his life that hadn't changed. Being a father came naturally to him, and he had slipped right back into the daddy role when returning home. Maybe because Riley was easygoing and didn't demand much. She loved to swim, loved to watch movies, loved to draw, and loved to eat.

Today they'd just hung out by the pool, Austin throwing her around or doing laps, and when Riley had wanted to paint, they'd gone up and settled on the terrace. Austin had read some more about Asperger's on his laptop; he'd also started four books, none of which had captured his attention. Meanwhile, Riley had been happily drawing and coloring at the table, and then they'd gone out for Mexican for lunch. Easy. So damn *easy*. But the rest of his life? No.

The newest thing was his odd fixation on Cam, but he was aware now that it was only his realization that was new. After all, they'd leaned on each other for months, and Austin had no problem admitting that he wanted to be close to Cam. It still felt weird not to wake up in the same room with him. Perhaps they argued heatedly—sometimes over nothing—but given the circumstances, it would be weird if they'd become all buddy-buddy right away in that metal cage. They'd had more important things to worry about—like staying alive.

Nevertheless, the thrill that had shot through Austin when he'd originally thought about Cam getting off to gay porn had now been identified.

It was excitement. Pure fucking excitement. Something that made him feel alive.

He should probably worry about that.

"Are your shoulders okay?" Angelo asked, yanking Austin back to now. "Any pain?"

"Everything's a pain," he grumbled and sat up. "When's our next session?"

"Oh, this isn't over yet, Huntley." Angelo smirked. "You say you're done; I say you're not." He pointed to the four exercise bikes by the mirrored wall. "Twenty minutes to work those thighs. Come on."

Austin bitched under his breath, grabbed his towel and water bottle, and followed the devil over to the bikes.

It all came down to control—again. Not being able to reach the goals set for him made him feel weak.

It had happened before.

"DAMN IT!" AUSTIN yelled, pushing himself off the floor. The fatigue was

getting to him, and it made him furious. No matter how much he worked out or how many times he pushed his own limits, he was getting weaker. Not stronger.

"Easy," Cam cautioned, still on the floor doing his sit-ups. "Take five then get back to it."

Before Austin could reply, the familiar sound of Psycho's arrival halted them. As he announced it was dinner time, Cam and Austin were quick to get rid of their clothes. Since the water was about to be changed and refilled, they used these brief moments to soak their underwear and T-shirts in the bucket, roughly scrubbing them with the bar of soap.

The days had long since started to blur together, and the men began to feel more like cattle than humans. Or wild animals. Unkempt, always hungry, restless, on edge, scared, caged, and weaker with each day that passed. Like moths, they were drawn to the poor light, and when the light was out, they moved around silently in the darkness.

There was little to no pride left, and there was no room for embarrassment or privacy. Everything happened with one man watching. Whether it was taking a shit or keeping emotions bottled up as they all missed their families, it all happened in front of a cellmate.

It was a psychological breakdown. Bit by bit, the madman in charge of their lives was stripping the guys of dignity, strength, and willpower.

It had been a while now since James had killed himself. Cam's bruises had yellowed and faded, and Chris, who'd been the last man to see the inside of the tiled interrogation room, was slowly recovering from his own battle wounds.

To Mr. Whoever-the-hell, Chris was named Thomas, and he'd apparently been their kidnapper's old boss. In comparison, Cam had been treated nicely. Pete, who shared a cell with Chris, had told the others that

Chris was completely bruised. From head to toe. He'd also cracked a few ribs, dislocated his shoulder, and broken a finger. It had taken days before Chris could even stand up.

Boredom and fear were a dangerous combination, and it was exactly what their captor pushed on to them. He left the ten—nine… the nine men to their own devices for days, only appearing to deliver food. Then he'd shake them up with torture and mind games. Sometimes he came down to announce a new name or wish them a happy Easter or "remember that it's Memorial Day," and he loved to play with the light switch. He said good morning when some men were sure it was closer to evening, and he said goodnight when a few others had just woken up.

The food remained the same. Chicken soup, stale bread, lukewarm milk, and new water for their buckets. Approximately once a week, a new roll of that sandpapery toilet paper was also tossed inside each cell.

Those who refused to carry out his commands, such as returning medical kits or putting on the cuffs again, had to go without food and water. In other words, it never took long for the men to admit defeat.

One day, the kidnapper was feeling nice. He gave the men toothbrushes and toothpaste.

It was a relief for the guys to clean their teeth with something other than soaped-up fingers or the sleeves of their shirts, but it hurt, too. Their gums were sore, some inflamed, and a couple men cursed about cracked fillings and cavities.

Not knowing exactly how long they'd been here made Austin go nuts. He was thinking about how quickly they were all deteriorating and wondered, realistically, how fast it could happen. The only thing each man was in agreement on was that it'd been more than two months now. Cam and Austin believed it had been more than three, too, but they couldn't be sure. Lance and

Victor thought they were approaching four months, but no others could imagine that to be true.

FUELED BY ANGER, Austin pushed himself to the limits on the bike. He needed routine back in his life, but that was pretty fucking hard to achieve when you didn't know what you wanted. Going back to work would be easy, but he reluctantly admitted to himself he wasn't ready to put in all those hours. So, what else was there? Because when he thought about it, there wasn't a whole lot more. Sure, there were the laps in the pool he did on weekends and a few weeknights; maybe he could make that a daily thing. Same went for waking up at the same hour every day and getting back to his morning routine—shower, shave, etcetera.

Then what?

There were a few things he did with Jade, but those felt stifling these days. He had no patience to sit down and watch a movie with her, because unlike Riley, who didn't really care if he was watching—as long as he sat next to her—Jade wanted his full attention on the movie so they could discuss it afterward. Dinner parties with their neighbors didn't appeal to him either, nor did he feel like taking his wife to plays and musicals. Actually, Austin had *never* enjoyed those things, but he'd never spoken up about it. They hadn't bothered him that much in the past. Content to be content—that was Austin. Until it wasn't anymore.

What was so wrong with just going to a bar to grab a beer? No, it had to be restaurants, wine, and a *fucking* show. Peanuts weren't enough; it had to be tiny appetizers with French names. God forbid if he wanted to stay home and catch a game. And he didn't have his old buddies left. Well, they were there, but there was no such thing as a guys' night. Everyone was paired up, and those who didn't live behind a picket fence had gates. You couldn't call up a friend and do something spontaneous, because the wife had to have a say, and babysitters had to be brought in.

He was bitter, but he didn't know if he had the right to be. There had been at least a hundred opportunities for him to speak up, yet he hadn't. Okay, he had suggested several things he'd wanted to do, and Jade had shut him down, but if he wanted it enough, perhaps he shouldn't have caved.

How had he allowed himself to become a doormat?

He had been that crazy bastard's torture toy, so maybe that was why he couldn't deal with not having the option to decide for himself anymore.

That was a lot of maybes. A lot to think about.

But right now, he wanted to get wasted. He wanted to go to a bar and just fucking drink.

Could he cancel dinner with the family just this once? He was expected to be home at seven—as always—but if he called Jade and said he just needed one night to himself, surely she'd understand *that*. He never denied Jade when she wanted to go to LA with her girlfriends for a day of shopping and spa treatments.

"Okay, Huntley. Let's walk it off on the treadmill."

Austin got off the bike, panting, and chugged down half a bottle of water.

He wondered if Angelo pushed Cam this hard. Or harder?

"Do you know any good bars in the area?" Austin stepped onto the treadmill, his legs feeling like jelly, but at least the hard part was over. Now he just had to walk for a bit, and then he had a half-hour massage.

"In Bakersfield?" Angelo gave him a dubious look and walked on the treadmill next to Austin's. "I suggest you go to LA for the weekend instead."

It had been a long time since Austin had gone to a bar, but come on. There were obviously plenty of places to go.

"There are a couple, but…" Angelo shrugged. "I don't know. I can text you the addresses."

"Huh." Austin decided to check more online once he was done here.

ACROSS TOWN, CAM squatted down and brushed his fingers over James's gravestone.

He had nothing to say. It wasn't a man he'd known; hell, he had never even seen the man's face, unless you counted the news articles with his photo. But it didn't really matter. There was a sense of camaraderie.

Pete's grave was also somewhere around here.

"MAIL CALL!"

Cam and Austin exchanged a look in the faint light and slowly stood up to see what the crazy motherfucker was up to this time.

It had been a quiet few days, and it felt like the calm before the storm.

When the hatch slid open, two envelopes were thrown inside before it closed again. The sound of more hatches opening echoed in the basement, and then silence. But… the douchebag hadn't left yet. They hadn't heard the footsteps on the stairs or the heavy door opening and closing.

Cam picked up his goddamn envelope and tried to keep his fingers from trembling. If weakness showed, he became angry. It caused his breathing to pick up, his mood to sour, and his thoughts to take a turn for the worse. First, his own reassurances would morph into worst-case scenarios, and then panic would settle.

Austin had seen it a few times now.

"What does it say in yours?" Austin asked, scanning his letter.

Cam scowled and read the three lines on the piece of paper. Three lines that told him the "company" was keeping him on board. "'Evan is a hard worker, but it's only a matter of time before he cracks,'" Cam muttered. "'For now, though, we're happy to have him with us.'"

Austin shook his head and dragged a hand over his scruffy jaw. It was itchy and irritating his skin. "Mine says almost the same." He sighed, then read a line to Cam. "'Sam has yet to show his potential, but we think he will. His position is safe for now.'"

They were quiet for a while before Psycho broke the silence.

"Dad!" he bellowed. "Read your letter for me!"

No answer.

"He's fuckin' crazy," Cam whispered, then took a deep breath to remain calm. If he lost it now, it wouldn't be pretty.

"Bill Stahl! Answer!"

Cam frowned, thinking about their characters. He had been referred to as their captor's cousin. Chris was his old boss. Now he was calling someone Dad... Bill Stahl.

"I'm—I'm Bill." Someone spoke up, his voice cracking. Cam was fairly positive it was Pete. He shared a cell with Chris.

"What does it say in your review?" Psycho asked impatiently.

Pete cleared his throat, the sound muffled by the layers of steel between them. "It says... it says, 'You are fired.'"

"That's right." Crazy laughed. "You're useless! And I'm sick—damn sick!—of how you've treated me, Dad! No goddamn respect!" A door was pushed open. "Ever since I was a teenager, you've favored Fred! Even Remy, that little queer!"

A shot rang out, blasting through the entire basement, and the ear-shattering sound stole Cam's and Austin's breaths.

"FUCK," CAM BREATHED out. He pressed his index finger and thumb to his eyes, as always struggling to remain calm. "Why the hell did I come here?" He was sure as shit starting to regret it. He should just head home to Bourbon instead. The pup shouldn't be left alone for long anyway.

He wanted to call Austin, but he refrained. He couldn't rely on him forever. Plus, he'd been thinking about that man too much today already.

Austin was probably at home with his family. It was dinnertime, and Cam could picture it. The all-American family. They probably had a nice house, perfect dinners together, movie nights, and played board games with Riley. Cam could definitely see that. Mr. MBA, the flawless father and husband. Jade certainly fit the role of a perfect wife with her statuesque figure, brilliant smile, blond hair, and blue eyes.

Lighting up a smoke, Cam sat down on the marble bench that looked new and just stared at the grave. If he wasn't so lazy, he'd look up Pete's spot. His death had hit him harder, mainly 'cause Pete hadn't chosen it.

"Motherfucker," he groaned as his heart began to race. No, he shouldn't have fucking come here.

CAM SAT ON his cot, arms wrapped around his drawn-up legs, and rocked back and forth. To keep sane, he tapped his thumb to his other fingers rapidly. Index, middle, ring, pinky. Pinky, ring, middle, index. Repeat. Pete was dead. Index, middle, ring, pinky. Repeat. That insane motherfucker had shot Pete in the head. Repeat. Repeat. Repeat.

No words were spoken in the basement, but it was far from quiet. Someone was vomiting, another one was crying without shame, Chris was banging on the walls of the cell he now shared with a dead man, Cam's fucking cuffs clanked together each time the pad of his thumb tapped a finger, and someone else was kicking things around.

"Breathe," Cam whispered to himself, close to hyperventilating. "Steady. Calm." He squeezed his eyes shut, angry at himself and his weakness—his flaws, his damaged brain. "Can't lose control. Can't lose control."

If his brother's wife heard him say shit like that, she would kick his ass. In truth, Cam knew his brain wasn't damaged, but goddamn... whatever. It sure as fuck felt like damage now.

"Cam."

Cam ignored his cellmate's voice and presence.

Austin sat down next to him. "Anything I can do?"

Fuck. He didn't even ask if something was wrong, 'cause a blind person would see that everything was wrong with Cam.

"We—we're outta c-control," Cam said between shallow breaths. "No control, no control. Fuck." His chest felt fucking tight. Another attack was on its way. "Nothing we can—nothing we can do. Nothing." Deserting his finger tapping, he fisted his hair and kept rocking.

Unbeknownst to him, Austin was worried sick. This kind of behavior wasn't... normal. "Hey, stop that." He tried to loosen Cam's hold on his dark, nearly black, hair. "Talk to me."

Cam responded as if Austin's request had been a command he had to obey, and he spoke words without really knowing what he was talking about. "My sister-in-law used to tell me that any disorder on the spectrum gives a person character. It's the shit that usually comes with Asperger's or whatever that makes it a challenge." Cam nodded. "Naïve. My sister-in-law was naïve. Still is, I guess. 'Cause she still says it sometimes. But I haven't seen her in... um, I don't know. I don't fucking know." He groaned.

Austin was speechless after Cam's verbal vomit, but eventually he found his words. "I'm sure there are more fitting words for your sister-in-law. But this disorder... Asperg—uh, what was it?

Cam sucked in a breath, slowly releasing his hair. "Asperger syndrome." He nodded again. "I used to say it was a lesser stupid than autism, but my mom whacked me on the head for saying that. She—she—" he swallowed dryly and tried to gather his jumbled thoughts "—she said I was stupid if I spoke stupid. She told me it made me come off as an idiot if I said shit that wasn't true."

"Uh." Austin cleared his throat, and it looked like he felt the need to tread carefully. "I've heard of Autism, but…" He released some air. "Does this Asperger syndrome cause your breathing problem?"

"No." Cam shook his head, slowing his rocking. "No. That's my anxiety disorder. It's what fucks me up." He tapped his temple. "I gotta be in control of my life. If I lose control, I panic. I don't fucking like it."

Austin didn't reply, appearing stunned.

"I'm not a fucking retard," Cam spat out defensively. "Before this, I hadn't had an attack in years. I don't like small spaces, I can't handle many people at the same time, I'm antisocial, I gotta have routines… but I ain't dumb." Cam's glare dared Austin to defy his words.

"Did I say you were dumb?" Austin arched a brow.

"I'm highly functioning." Cam went on as if Austin hadn't said a word. "I was behind when I was a kid, but that's fucking it. So what if I didn't speak 'til I was four?" He scowled at the floor. "And so what if I don't like people?"

Again, Austin failed to respond.

"Don't treat me any different just 'cause you know now," Cam finished in a mutter.

"I won't," Austin murmured.

WHEN CAM BEGAN to hyperventilate, he called Landon instead. He was sick of Austin seeing him this way.

EIGHT

ON FRIDAY, AUSTIN found himself watching the clock as they ate an early dinner.

Jade hadn't liked the idea of Austin going to a bar after his session with Angelo a few days ago, and she had flat out refused to let him skip dinner. So, they'd come to a compromise. He could go out today when Jade had plans to take Riley to visit her parents in Delano. They were spending the weekend, too, so that was that.

"All done!" Riley declared and pushed the plate away from her. "Can I watch some TV before we go?"

"Of course," Austin said as Jade said, "No."

Riley scrunched her nose and watched her parents as they stared at each other.

"We eat together," Jade insisted. "It's how it's always been."

Austin refused to cave, though. While keeping his gaze fixed on Jade, he told Riley, "You're excused, baby girl. Just put your plate in the dishwasher first."

Riley quietly thanked them for dinner and put the plate in the dishwasher before she quickly escaped the tension building in the kitchen.

"What the hell, Austin?" Jade gritted out. "It's like you're not you anymore."

"I'm not!" he whisper-shouted. "How many times do I have to tell you that?" He had tried. God, had he tried. Mostly after his sessions with Gale, he had come home wanting to talk about them, but Jade didn't want to hear it. She reluctantly listened until she could find some emergency to deal with. "I've told you I feel different, that I need time—"

"I want my husband back," Jade said as her eyes welled up. "You were taken from me, and now that you're home again, you're still not you."

Austin felt like he was talking to a brick wall. "You're not listening to me, Jade." He lowered his voice and tried to be patient, but it wasn't easy with all that anger bottled up inside. "I can't *help* it." He placed a hand on his chest. "I need time to readjust, and things *will* be different—"

"But I don't want it to be different!" she cried. "I want us to have what we used to have. I want us to go back to normal. But you won't do that." She wiped away some tears. "You're always on edge, you can't sit still—it feels like I'm walking on eggshells around you!"

Austin shook his head, at a loss. Yeah, he was on edge—constantly—but he had never done anything to make Jade feel frightened, or as she said, walk on eggshells. He tried to do her bidding as much as he could in order to "go back to normal," but it wasn't working.

"I'm not a magician," he said quietly. "I can't snap my fingers and forget what I've been through. What you're asking is too much."

"Then we have a problem," Jade choked out.

"Are you serious?" Austin couldn't believe how cold she was being. "After fifteen years together, you can't even support me on this?"

It made him question why he was even sitting here having this discussion. He needed time to gather his thoughts, to find out what it was he wanted for himself, but it clearly wouldn't be his own wife if she was hell-bent on having the old Austin back. To her, it seemed like it was all or nothing.

"I'm sorry," she whimpered, looking guilty for some reason. "But I'm struggling, too, Austin. And I can't handle this."

"You haven't even tried!" he replied furiously. "We haven't talked about *shit*, Jade." He was getting riled up. "You've been offered counseling, just like the other family members, and you turned that down. *I* have tried to talk to you about what I've been through, and what *you've* been through, but you shut that down, too." Shaking his head, he stood up and threw the napkin on the table. "I'll go talk to Riley, then I'm leaving."

Maybe a weekend alone was just what he needed.

Saying goodbye to Riley wasn't easy. She tried to convince him to come with them to Gramma and Grampa, but he couldn't. The more he thought about it, the more he realized time on his own might help. He did promise to call her though, and they made plans to go to LA together next week. "We'll head out early in the morning, spend the day on the beach, and then we'll come home late," he told her, which made her smile again.

WHEN AUSTIN ARRIVED at the bar Angelo had suggested, he knew what he was getting into. It was clear now that Angelo thought he was gay, because after checking online, Austin found out this bar was one of the very few gay-friendly places to go in Bakersfield.

It was a dive bar, and a small live band was playing when Austin sat down at the end of the bar and ordered a beer. It didn't... look... like a gay bar. The floor was sticky, a few older guys were occupying the pool table, a couple younger girls were squealing at... something... and the crowd seemed to be into the bluesy rock the band was playing. But what the hell did he know? Austin had never been to a gay bar before, but he wanted to come here tonight.

He wondered if Cam had been here.

Yeah, he couldn't stop thinking about that man. They hadn't spoken in days, and Austin was afraid Cam was avoiding him. To escape the risk of rejection, Austin hadn't reached out. Which ultimately made him wonder if he was in high school. An almost forty-year-old man should probably call Cam up and clear the air—if that was necessary.

Subtly glancing around him, Austin sipped his beer and thought about the stupidest shit: who was gay and who wasn't.

When others looked at him, did they wonder the same? Probably not. He felt ridiculous. And self-conscious. He was dressed in a pair of dark jeans and a gray button-down; nothing weird with that, right?

"This seat taken?"

Tilting his head, Austin saw a man watching him. "No. Go ahead."

The man was younger, probably by ten years or so, and he was… fine, he was attractive. Austin could admit that. Maybe a bit too boyish, though. Blond, blue-eyed, slender, and more cute than sexy—

What the fuck was going on with him? Austin found himself questioning everything, but at the same time, he was fairly accepting of anything new. He just wished he could understand it. He wanted something concrete to stick to.

"I'm Brian." The man stuck out his hand and smiled.

Austin nodded with a dip of his chin and shook his hand. "Austin."

Brian's smile brightened. "Nice to see a new face around here. But… you do look familiar. Have I seen you somewhere before?" His eyes raked over Austin's body, making him slightly uncomfortable. "Hmm. Married, are we?" He eyed the ring on Austin's finger.

"Yes."

Brian hummed and took a sip from his own beer. "Love is a bitch. I'm trying to get over mine."

"Really." It wasn't a question. Austin was in way over his head, and he wondered if maybe he'd been out of the bar scene for too long. Not that it had ever really been his scene, but in his college years, he did go out occasionally—when his roommate had managed to drag him out.

"Yeah, so I should probably stop texting him." Brian sighed wistfully. "He's this broody kind of guy, bad-boyish with a leather jacket to match—the one you'll hopelessly fall for, all while knowing he just sees you as a casual fuck-buddy." Well, if there was any question about Brian's sexual preferences, Austin just received the confirmation. "I knew it wasn't gonna last, and we weren't exclusive or anything, but..." He waved a hand. "So, anyway, what brings you here? Meeting someone?"

Austin shook his head no. "Just wanted to go out for a beer." Or fourteen.

"You've come to the right place, then!" Brian's bright smile was back. "I'm actually a bartender here, but it's my day off." Facing the bar, he yelled to someone named Christina, and she appeared right away. "Honey, how about some shots for us?" He turned to Austin again. "What's your poison, handsome?"

Fuck beer, Austin decided. "Jäger, thanks." He'd go for bourbon, but that was meant to be savored. Not downed.

"A man's man." Brian winked. "I love it. I'll have tequila. Christina honey, you know what I like."

Soon, both men had shots lined up, and Christina had left the bottles with them. Not very wise, but whatever.

"OKAY, I THINK I have you figured out now," Brian slurred and pointed a wobbly finger in Austin's face.

Austin chuckled and threw back another shot. His new friend could not handle his liquor, that was for certain. Granted, Austin was definitely drunk, but he could still stand straight. Brian was three sheets to the wind.

"You're married to a woman," Brian stated, and Austin nodded. "But you're not here for the cheap drinks. And I think— yes, I think you're bi-curious. Am I close?"

Austin smiled and shrugged, as if to say, *"Maybe. Maybe not."*

He honestly didn't know, because there had never been anyone to tell him that a man couldn't appreciate another man's good looks. He hadn't known that meant gay to some.

Over the years, he had found many men attractive, but that didn't mean he wanted to fuck them. With the booze flowing, however, it was easier to confess to himself that sometimes he wanted to get so close to Cam that he'd be under the man's skin. The morning he'd woken up wrapped around Cam… that had felt so fucking *right*. It had been thrilling as well as comforting.

"It's too bad you're married, honey." Brian leaned close and put a hand on Austin's thigh. "I would've *loved* to show you some stuff."

Austin laughed and was about to say something, but a man bumped into Brian from behind and spat out, "Get a fucking room, cocksuckers."

"Oh!" Some of the guys around the bar erupted.

Austin saw red, but before he could even react, a flashback nearly knocked him over.

"FINISH THE DAMN food, Cam," Austin said impatiently. *"You're never going to be able to keep up your strength if you don't eat."*

"Shut the fuck up, cocksucker."

Austin gritted his teeth and chugged the last of his soup straight out of the bowl. It'd been like this for the past few days—ever since Cam had revealed his disorder, that Asperger whatever-it-was. Cam had been defensive, hostile, and cursing more than he usually did. He'd also returned to sitting on his cot doing nothing. No more working out, no eating properly; it was like Cam had shut down.

It infuriated Austin as well as it worried him. If he was ever going to see his daughter again, he needed Cam to be alert. They needed strength—it always came down to that. If they dissolved into nothing, they wouldn't be able to fight. They had to keep hoping that an opportunity would arise, and if… when it did, they had to be ready.

More often than not, their sleep was disrupted by cries and shouts. Nightmares had become a given as soon as they shut their eyes. Chris, especially, who was still sharing his cell with a corpse.

"Nothing to say, huh?" Cam chuckled darkly. *"Maybe that means it's true. You're a cocksucker."*

Austin flew up from his cot, crossed the small cell, and yanked Cam up by the collar of his filthy T-shirt. With a furious glare, he stared down the younger man who was a few inches shorter than his six four.

"You think acting like a high school bully makes you cool?" He tightened his grip on Cam's shirt. *"You think it makes you look strong?"*

"Get your fucking hands off me," Cam seethed and grabbed at Austin's forearms. *"You don't know who the fuck you're dealin' with."*

Austin laughed and shoved him away—roughly. "I know a pathetic jerk when I see one. You want to be a dick? Fine." He looked down at Cam, who'd ended up on the floor, in disgust. "If you're so strong and smart—" leaning down, he stabbed a finger at Cam's forehead "—use that anger to do something useful instead."

Cam said nothing; he just glared up at Austin.

AUSTIN SHOOK HIS head quickly, feeling dizzy from both the flashback and the alcohol, and got up on his feet. He faced the bastard who needed to learn some goddamn manners and seethed. "What the fuck did you just say?" Grabbing onto the bartop, he steadied himself.

"Just calm down now," Brian cautioned. "There's always one bad egg—come on, Austin. Christina's already called the bouncer."

"I think you heard me the first time, fag," the man said with a smirk.

Austin Huntley had finally found a physical outlet for all his anger.

NINE

CAM KNEW HOW important discipline was for dogs, so if he allowed Bourbon in the bed one time, he'd have to struggle all the more later when he weighed seventy pounds. It wouldn't be so precious to have Bourbon up there then. Also, what if he was jostled awake one night by a puppy but automatically thought it was Psycho?

So... Cam sat on the floor right now, leaning back against the bed, and had his little puppy goofing around on his lap with a new chew toy while Cam watched a movie on the flat screen.

The past few days had been exhausting for Cam, so this was all he wanted this Friday. Peace and quiet. Okay, that was a fucking lie; there was something else he wanted, but that would only lead to trouble. He needed to distance himself from Austin before... *before what?* Before Cam craved him more? He doubted he could want Austin more than he already did.

It wasn't purely physical, although the man had become the biggest star in his morning showers, but it was the companionship that he wanted the most. Even if they bickered like old women sometimes.

Sighing, he glanced at his phone on the low coffee table in front of him, and he debated... one text wouldn't hurt—just to check in, to see how he was doing... but the dude could be asleep. A family man like him probably went to bed around nine. He snorted to himself and looked down at Bourbon who was chewing the shit out of that toy.

"Christ!" He nearly jumped out of his own skin when the phone rang. Bourbon barked, which was cute, not threatening, and Cam picked up his phone and made a face when he recognized the number. "Dammit."

He had erased Brian from his contact list, but he still remembered parts of the number. Mainly 'cause he'd been screwing the guy on and off for a year before he was kidnapped, but also 'cause Brian had texted him a few times in the past couple days.

Cam hadn't replied, but now he had to. "Yeah?" he muttered and reached for his beer.

"Cam!" That was Brian, all right. *"Is there any way you could pick me up? Phil won't give me my keys."* Now there was a pout in his voice, which just annoyed Cam. He'd never really liked guys who acted like women, but it hadn't bothered him when Brian's mouth was full of his cock. *"I really wouldn't have called you if there was anyone else."*

"Fuck," Cam groaned in defeat. "It's midnight. You don't think I got better shit to do?"

"I can make it up to you!"

Cam rolled his eyes and moved Bourbon off his lap. "I'm sure you can. Why won't Phil give you your keys?" He had met up with Brian where he worked a few times, so he knew the bouncer a little. Enough to know that Phil usually didn't give a flying fuck about who was too drunk to drive.

"There may have been a fight," Brian said pitifully. *"I'm fine! But Phil says I shouldn't drive."*

Cam sighed and got off the floor. "I'll be there in ten, idiot."

CAM PULLED UP outside the bar in his Dodge and grabbed the beanie from the dashboard. He looked like a fucking bum in baggy cargo pants, a long-sleeved T-shirt, and the surfer-dude hair that he hid under the beanie, but he was only here to play designated driver. Lighting up a smoke, he left the car and fired off a text to Brian that said he was here now.

"Cam?"

He spun around, only to see Austin ten feet away, leaning back against the building with his phone in hand. They frowned at each other, both surprised, and then Cam noticed the cut on Austin's eyebrow and approached.

"What the fuck happened?" He didn't stop until he was right in front of Austin. "Why are you here?" *Of all places*, he wanted to add.

Reaching up, he adjusted Austin's glasses then touched the bruise forming on his jaw. The man had obviously been in a fight, but he still looked good. Damn good. Sexy, even.

Fuuuck.

"Angelo thinks I'm gay," Austin answered dumbly. It caused Cam's eyebrows to shoot up. "I wanted to go out—he said I should go to LA instead. But he mentioned this place, so…"

"And that gave you bruises," Cam said sarcastically. He took a step back and inhaled from his smoke. Being close to this man was easy, but it wasn't right. It made Cam want more. He felt so fucking drawn to him.

"No, just…" Austin muttered something under his breath. "Some asshole wanted trouble. I let him know what I thought about it." He took a seemingly unconscious step toward Cam.

"Does he look worse?" Cam's mouth quirked up. Not for one second did he doubt Austin's strength. Yeah, he came off as a straitlaced family man, but Cam knew better.

"Damn right," Austin chuckled and touched his bottom lip. "He left a while ago."

Cam followed the movement before he looked away and cleared his throat. "So, you ended up at a gay bar by mistake, huh?" He took another pull and flicked away some ash.

Austin's eyes were intense, and there was something hidden in that gaze. Almost as if Cam was supposed to read between the lines. Then that intensity morphed into an obvious nervousness, and Austin took yet another step closer. "No." They looked down on the few inches that separated them as Austin reached for the hem of Cam's shirt. He just fidgeted with it loosely, brushing his thumb over the soft fabric. "I looked it up before I came here."

"Oh." Cam swallowed and briefly closed his eyes. He was

close enough now to smell Austin, and he fought a shiver. "So, uh…" He wet his lips, his eyes flicking up to Austin's face. So close. "Why—"

He wanted to finish his fucking question about why Austin had gone to a gay bar, but Brian chose that moment to interrupt.

"My savior!" Brian dramatically clung to Cam's arm, as he reluctantly stepped away from Austin. "I'm ready to go home— oh, Austin!" He grinned, then frowned, then frowned deeper. "Do you two know each other?"

"Yeah," Cam replied, uncomfortable and irritated. He moved away from Brian. "He and I were… I mean, Austin was also one of the guys who was kidnapped."

"Oh!" Brian gasped. "That's why you looked so familiar." He nodded sadly and touched Austin's exposed forearm. "I read about you in the papers."

"Right." Austin was uncomfortable, too. "Well, uh, I should call a cab—"

"Fuck that." Cam had a chance to see Austin; he would make the most of it. He just had to get rid of Brian first. "I'll drive you." He jerked his chin toward his car. "We'll drop off Brian first, then I can take you home."

"But…" Brian looked a bit put out. "Maybe we should take Austin home first, and then—"

Cam didn't catch Austin's scowl that he directed at the ground.

"You live five minutes away from here." Cam grew impatient and started walking to his car. "Come on." As he threw away his cigarette, he noticed that Austin wasn't putting a lot of pressure on his left leg, and that worried him. "You okay?" He cupped Austin's elbow to support him, remembering how Psycho had injured him in the first place. If someone had made it worse inside that bar, Cam wanted to hunt that motherfucker down and rearrange his face.

"It's nothing." Austin grimaced, swallowed his pride, and allowed Cam to help him.

THE RIDE TO Brian's apartment building was pretty quiet. He didn't look happy about sitting in the back while Austin sat in the front next to Cam, but what-the-fuck-ever. Cam had been honest from the beginning; it was just sex. Now it was over. End of story. But Cam wasn't stupid. He could see that Austin had gotten in the way of Brian's plans. As if Cam wouldn't say no if they'd been alone. Fucking ridiculous.

"Thanks for picking me up." Brian sighed softly as they arrived at his place. "Maybe we can meet up sometime, Cam?"

Cam just gave him a look in the rearview mirror. He didn't wanna be a dick, but he had more important shit going on in his life.

"Fine. Be that way." Brian offered a bitchface in return, then got out of the car. "It was nice meeting you, Austin."

"You too." Austin nodded curtly. And once Cam pulled away from the sidewalk again, he shifted in his seat. "So, you're the guy who got away."

Cam side-eyed him. "What?"

"Brian came up to me in that bar—said he was trying to get over the guy he loved or something. And coupled with his description, I'm guessing it's you."

Oh, *this* Cam wanted to hear. "What description would that be? By the way, tell me where to drive." He didn't know exactly where Austin lived.

"Are you tired?" Austin asked. "Jade and Riley are in Delano over the weekend, and I really don't feel like going home."

"My place it is." Cam made a sharp turn. "Now, that description?"

Austin had an odd look, as if something wasn't quite right. "I think he used the words broody, bad-boyish—" Cam grunted, to which Austin laughed quietly "—and apparently there's a leather jacket to go with your attitude."

Cam rolled his eyes, and it got quiet for a beat or two.

Then Austin asked hesitantly, "Is he an ex?"

"I wouldn't go that far." He shook his head. "We met up occasionally at his place. It was casual."

Austin hummed, now appearing guarded. "Yeah, he mentioned that. But to him it wasn't."

There wasn't a whole lot Cam could say in response to that, so he said nothing. For a while. Then he wanted to retract something he'd said days ago. "That's why I have my rule. I don't bring people home to fuck. If I did, I'd have memories to haunt me forever." He shuddered at the truth of that.

Cam could feel Austin's eyes on him for a while, though he pretended not to notice. Instead he pressed on the gas a little and sighed in contentment when he drove on to his street.

Bourbon greeted them in the hallway, and Cam groaned at the sight of more piss on the floor.

"Not cool, little guy." He bent down to scratch Bourbon behind his ears. "I took you for an hour-long walk after dinner." Plus, there was a doggy door now that led to the patio, and the pool had been covered. Straightening, he told Austin, "You know where the bathroom is if you wanna shower." He gestured at the stains of alcohol on his button-down and—*shit*. "Is that blood?" He closed the distance and touched Austin's ribcage.

"Not my own," he replied quickly. "But I'll take that shower. I smell like the damn bar."

Cam nodded, frowning, and stepped back. He hated seeing his friend injured. "There're towels in there, new toothbrushes under the sink, and I'll find you something to wear." Austin thanked him and headed toward the hallway where Cam's bedroom, workout room, and bathroom were. He still wasn't putting pressure on his left leg. "Do you need any help, man?"

"No, it's okay. Thanks." Austin disappeared down the hall.

While he showered, Cam cleaned up the mess Bourbon had left him, then went to the kitchen and stood by the window and smoked a cigarette. He had promised himself no more smoking in the living room—for Bourbon's sake—and only by the kitchen window when it was dark out. Eventually, when he got over his embarrassing fear of darkness, he'd go out on the patio even at night.

After using the half-bath in the hallway to freshen up, he ended up in his bedroom where he grabbed a pair of sweats that were a size too large for Cam. He also picked out boxers, which felt odd, and a T-shirt. He didn't know what Austin slept in, but he'd slept in sweats the last time he was here. He'd also gone commando—something Cam should probably forget.

Lastly, he changed into a pair of black basketball shorts to sleep in, and then he knocked on the bathroom door in the hall, told Austin his change of clothes was right outside, and returned to the living room.

By the time Austin appeared, Cam was idly playing with his cell phone and there was a bad movie playing in the background.

"Mind if I dim the lights?" Austin stopped in the doorway, one hand on the switch.

Cam waved a hand in *go ahead* then looked away, wondering about Austin's aversion to clothes. He was only wearing the sweatpants, not the shirt, and not the fucking boxers. It was way too easy to tell.

With the lights dimmed low, Austin joined Cam on the bed, but instead of sitting down next to him, Austin scooted farther in and lay down on the pillow.

"Tired?" Cam twisted his upper body and looked behind him. Austin really did look exhausted, and he wondered if the last days had been as taxing for him as they had for Cam.

"Like you wouldn't believe." Austin reached up on the partition wall above him and placed his glasses there. Cam noticed that the bandages around Austin's wrists had been removed. There was scarring, but it wasn't too bad. "I'll be glad when this week is over."

"Did something happen?" Cam shut off the TV and pulled the soft blanket over them, lying on his side next to Austin.

This time there were two pillows, and he didn't know if that was a good thing or bad. Ending up close happened so naturally, so the lines blurred easily. There was no thought about offering the couch in his bedroom to Austin, 'cause they slept together. It was how it had been for several nights in captivity.

"Mostly today," Austin sighed as they shifted closer to one another. In the end, as had become common for the two men, they were close enough so their foreheads touched. "I'm pretty sure I see divorce on the horizon."

"What the fuck?" Cam's eyes widened. "I didn't even know you had problems." He was genuinely shocked, and as the news settled, he pushed away any thoughts of what this could mean—*for him.*

"Neither did I," Austin chuckled mirthlessly. "Well…" He hesitated. "That was a lie. We've had problems, but I didn't know they were this big. I don't know." He heaved a sigh and looked down between them. "In the past few years, we've just been going through the motions. Then all this shit happened, and now she's… it's like she's looking for a way out." He faced Cam again. "She said she can't deal with the aftermath of what I've been through, but I think it's more than that."

Cam frowned, at a loss. He didn't know enough about Austin's marriage to say a single thing. It was something they didn't talk about, not even in captivity. Cam had never asked in that cell, 'cause he'd sensed it had been a topic that made Austin feel worse. And when Austin offered to share stories, they were mainly about Riley, his parents, stuff from his childhood… one time he even told Cam who Riley was named after.

As the silence stretched on, the subject died, and Austin looked content where he was. That comforted Cam a little, and he hoped the dude was all right. Perhaps he should ask him about it, but he honestly didn't want to. He wasn't very good with words, and he had no desire to listen to Austin go on about the woman he presumably loved.

"I wasn't lying when I said you're the only one who makes sense to me," Austin murmured after a while. He cleared his throat and averted his eyes once more. "I mean, Gale helps, but... it's not the same thing."

Cam nodded slowly and instinctively moved his hand up Austin's arm, wanting to comfort. And to be closer. And to touch. And to fucking *have*. "I know." He did know. Since he last saw Austin days ago, he'd had two sessions with Gale, and she *was* good, but like Austin said, it wasn't the same. She hadn't been in that cell with him.

As Austin tilted up his face again, their noses touched. Cam sucked in a breath, his heart suddenly pounding in his ribcage. He held that breath while Austin closed the distance between their bodies and wrapped an arm around his middle.

"Austin..." What the fuck was he doing?

Cam got his answer the second Austin brushed his lips over Cam's. Shallow breaths were exchanged while their mouths stayed connected in a ghosting touch. It was light, barely there, but fucking electrifying. When Austin applied pressure, Cam groaned in surrender and deepened the kiss further. He parted his lips and swiped the tip of his tongue over Austin's bottom lip. In return, Austin let out a quiet moan and pushed his tongue into Cam's mouth.

Their kiss grew greedier and greedier, as did their hands. No longer shying away from the blurry line of what was appropriate and not, Cam slid his hands down to Austin's firm ass and pulled him closer and closer until he could grind their hardening cocks together.

"Jesus," Austin panted. He broke away from the kiss to catch his breath, but he was back soon, only more eager in his movements. Hitching a leg over Cam's hip, he pushed himself up and ended on top. "Should I stop?" He nipped at Cam's scruffy jaw, then claimed him in another deep kiss.

"Only if you're a fucking idiot." Cam grunted and stuck his hands down Austin's sweatpants.

His blunt fingernails dug into the flesh of Austin's ass, causing him to groan and thrust his hips forward. *Fuck*, that felt good. He wasn't about to get sentimental like some pussy, but there was no denying how satisfying this was on every damn level known to man. Not only was Austin sexy, but he was a good man—and an intoxicating kisser.

They kissed hard, deeply, tongues mingling, teeth nipping, and warm lips fusing. The scuff rasped tantalizingly, and it only made Cam's dick harder.

He needed to take the lead, though. Cam had no idea what was going on in Austin's head—and what had gone in there for the past few days, maybe even longer. But while the man seemed perfectly at ease with the kissing and teenage-style dry humping, Cam could sense Austin's hesitation about taking it further.

"Let me get you off." Cam's voice was gritty with lust as he rolled them over. In that metal cage they'd shared, they had seen each other naked countless times, but it hadn't been like this. "Lose the pants, Austin." Cam dipped down and kissed him sensually, slowly, still deeply, while Austin pushed down his sweats. Then Cam let his right hand slide down to Austin's thick cock. They both shuddered. "Fuck," he breathed out. His fingers wrapped around the smooth, heavy, and steel-hard dick.

"Cam," Austin moaned. Cam stroked him teasingly, wishing he had lube nearby. Unlike him, Austin was circumcised. "Oh Christ, so good."

Cam hummed and captured Austin's mouth in a kiss, then moved his own mouth farther down. He took his time, kissing the hard planes of Austin's chest. He smelled fucking amazing, and Cam wanted to worship this body. It was a new feeling.

Settling between Austin's legs, Cam nudged them farther apart and spent some time kissing his abs, muscular thighs, and the trimmed area around his cock. His own dick was pressing against the mattress, needing friction, which made him curious as to how far Austin was willing to take this.

Burying his nose at the root of Austin's cock, he breathed in deeply, groaning at the musky scent of bodywash and arousal. His mouth watered. He moaned, and he fisted the cock harder and licked his way up the underside of it. Then he closed his mouth over the head, suckling and gently grazing it with his teeth.

"Oh, fuck." Austin let out a whimpered breath and threaded his fingers through Cam's hair. Not really guiding him—just wanting him down there. As Cam wet his lips and started sucking, he looked up to find Austin watching him with hunger and deep-rooted desire in his eyes.

Wanting to take the next step, Cam paused for a second—never breaking their gaze—and coated the tip of his thumb in saliva, then took Austin's entire length into his mouth again. The head touched the back of Cam's throat, and a small spurt of pre-come spread its flavor in his mouth. He closed his eyes and moaned around Austin's cock; at the same time, he slid his thumb down to Austin's ass. The last thing he wanted was to take it too far, but he had a feeling Austin would enjoy this.

"Jesus Christ, don't stop, Cam." Austin threw his head back on the pillow, his body tense with pleasure. He even pulled his knees up and farther apart, exposing himself to Cam. "So fucking good," he groaned as Cam circled his hole with the pad of his thumb.

He brushed over it softly, drawing out the experience. In the meantime, he tightened his lips around Austin's dick and sucked harder, took him deeper, and sped up.

Every now and then, in small pulses, Cam tasted Austin's arousal. It drove him fucking mad with lust. He breathed through his nose, intent on giving Austin all he had—focus, attention, a good fucking orgasm. He took all of Austin's cock and sucked 'til his jaw ached. One hand teased his ass, going from stroking and rubbing to pushing and slowly pressing inside. His other hand cupped Austin's tight sac, massaging and tugging.

"Close," Austin eventually choked out. "*Fuck*—I'm coming."

If his body was tense before, it had nothing on this.

Cam watched the defined muscles of Austin's torso as his orgasm took over. The first release hit the back of his throat just as the last inch of Cam's thumb disappeared into Austin's ass. Austin moaned and grunted, fisting Cam's hair to keep him where he was. Not that Cam had plans to leave yet. He swallowed everything, gently fucking him with his thumb, and didn't stop until Austin shuddered and unclenched his muscles.

Both were panting as Cam kissed his way up Austin's body again, one in need, one in obvious exertion.

Cam wasn't gonna lie and say some kissing and cuddling would do; he fucking needed to get off. How was the only question.

But Austin didn't appear to have plans to leave him hanging. When they were face-to-face again, Austin took control of the kiss. Their tongues met, and Cam was almost caught off guard by the possessiveness with which Austin kissed him.

He surrendered willingly, ending up on his back with Austin half on top of him and running the show. His left hand explored Cam's chest, and it was almost tender. So fucking sensual.

"I didn't like seeing Brian so close to you," Austin admitted out of nowhere. "I have no right to feel that, but…" He didn't allow Cam to answer right away, kissing him hard.

Cam flushed with heat and pulled Austin closer, reveling in the feeling of being claimed. *God-fucking-dammit, he's sexy.* He felt like he was being seduced, which Cam considered a form of foreplay he rarely engaged in. He'd had his hookups, and all he'd ever needed was a phone call to confirm. There hadn't been a man or a woman in Cam's life for a long time where he hadn't gone the fuck-and-duck route.

"He's outta the picture," Cam muttered breathlessly as Austin dragged his short fingernails over Cam's chest. "And you're killing me here." His nipples were fucking sensitive, making the skin around his cock tighten each time Austin touched him. And the kisses didn't stop, either. Whether it was on the lips or down his neck, Austin's mouth didn't leave his body. "Shit." He exhaled and shivered as Austin's hand trailed down to Cam's abs.

"No patience?" Austin smiled into the kiss he dropped on Cam's sternum. By now, Austin's fingers were dipping under the waistband of Cam's basketball shorts.

"Overrated," Cam grunted. He lifted his head and kissed the side of Austin's neck. The smell of sex was heavy in the air, and it was as addictive as Austin himself. "Oh fuck, yeah." Cam collapsed down onto the pillow again as Austin finally fisted his hard cock. "Keep going." He reached down and squirmed his way out of his shorts and boxer briefs.

Once Cam was completely naked, Austin positioned himself on top of him, lining up his half-hard cock with Cam's throbbing one. They moaned. Austin stroked them both at a steady pace, all while he returned to kiss whatever spot on Cam's body he could reach. The man seemed to have a thing for Cam's ink, as he often lingered there.

There were words left unsaid between the men—Cam could feel it. But maybe they weren't ready for that shit. Words sometimes complicated things.

"Don't you use anything when you jerk off?" Austin asked, looking down between them. "Lotion or whatever."

Cam pushed his hips forward, sliding his cock deeper into Austin's hold. "Does it look like I need it?" That was for men who were cut. Grasping Austin's chin, Cam pulled him in for a hard kiss. They moved together, two cocks rubbing against one another in Austin's hand. "Yeah, that's it." Cam moaned.

Austin was spreading a bead of pre-come over them, making the friction slicker and hotter. Next he let go completely, but before Cam could protest, Austin licked his palm and resumed jerking them.

Austin smirked and kissed Cam's jaw. "Better?"

"Yeah." Cam nodded, feeling his balls tightening. His abs tensed. A slow burn spread throughout his body, and he started to pant. "Fuck, Austin." That name went on a loop in his head as he got closer and closer to his climax. Goddamn, he was desperate to get off now.

Without warning, Cam went rigid. Heat shot down his spine toward his groin, and it felt like his balls were gonna explode. He came with a groan, soaking them in three, four streams. Austin gathered what he caught and used it as lube, prolonging Cam's orgasm by squeezing them together harder. Cam was nearly blinded by the white-hot fire that flashed before his eyes. Austin's passionate kisses and moans only made it better.

"Fuck!" Cam gasped as his body finally relaxed. He melted into the mattress, feeling like he was made out of jelly. "God…" He swallowed, his kisses lazy and messy. "You ready for more?" He could feel that Austin was hard again.

"No," Austin chuckled drowsily, collapsing next to him. "I'm not twenty anymore." He hummed and pulled Cam close, obviously not giving a shit about the cooling release between them. "Damn, I'm tired."

"Me too." And maybe Austin didn't care about the mess, but Cam did. "I'll be right back."

He disappeared for a minute, then returned with a washcloth. He'd already wiped himself clean, and now he zeroed in on Austin's naked body. Shit, he really was a sight. He was more tan than Cam, and in the dim light of the living room, Austin's skin looked almost golden.

"Good service," Austin murmured, his smile more evident in his eyes than on his lips.

"Don't get used to it." Cam laughed through his nose and shook his head. He finished and threw the washcloth in the laundry before getting back into bed. "By the way—" he stifled a yawn and slid under the blanket, into Austin's waiting arms "—if you wake up tomorrow regretting this, you know where the fucking door is."

He'd said it as a joke, but he felt the truth of the statement.

"You have nothing to worry about." Austin kissed him chastely, as if it was the most natural thing in the world, and wrapped an arm around Cam's waist. "I promise."

Unfortunately, Cam wasn't so sure. His mind was already spinning. While he knew Austin was still intoxicated, he wasn't drunk off his ass. Austin had wanted this. But maybe he was under the influence enough to ignore the obvious consequences that were about to follow. Too many things had to be taken into consideration—or rather, people. Not things. Austin's wife. Riley. Then his and Cam's friendship.

Now, Cam wasn't some nagging woman who had to overanalyze everything, but he did need to have his facts straight.

Whatever had happened tonight couldn't be taken lightly. It would change shit.

Cam fucking hated changes.

TEN

WHEN AUSTIN WOKE up the morning after, he'd expected to find Cam next to him. He'd also been ready to calm him down in case he attacked Austin like he had on the patio last week. But Cam wasn't there. He was in the kitchen; Austin could hear pots and pans clanking together with unnecessary force. Cupboards, too. And there was the fridge door. Or freezer.

With a sigh, Austin rolled onto his back and stared up at the ceiling. He didn't know what to think—what to feel—about last night, this week... hell, his life. It would be damn easy to push it all down and ignore it—for a while—but it couldn't go on forever. Eventually, he'd have to figure out what he wanted.

Thinking about Jade didn't help with his anger, although he didn't really have a choice. Austin loathed the fact that he'd technically cheated on his own wife, but... He'd felt betrayed by her words; she'd basically given him an ultimatum. Then on the other hand, he didn't know if he really cared anymore. About their marriage, about *her*.

Because what had started out as craving comfort from Cam had morphed into an indescribable attraction.

Yesterday he hadn't been able to control himself. He'd thought about Cam too much, and then when he'd connected the dots between Brian and Cam… it had turned him into a jealous bastard who needed to mark his territory. He'd felt threatened.

He had no regrets whatsoever about last night, but he probably could've gone about it differently. Like when he had his shit together. Not when he was drunk, probably-or-maybe getting divorced, tired, confused, and weak.

Austin felt weak now, too. In fact, he felt like he could break down. It was all becoming too much. While half his mind was ready to shut down and become a robot, the other half of him was screaming. His breathing sped up. His head was swimming. He was slightly hungover. A headache began to settle in. He didn't know what was going to happen today. He didn't know what he had left.

There was no control.

If day-by-day doesn't work, take it hour-by-hour. What do you want, Austin?

Gale's question went on repeat, and he asked himself the same. What did he want?

It was too soon to say exactly what it was with Cam that Austin wanted, and he wanted to break it down to just a one-word answer: Cam. He wanted Cam—*needed* Cam—period, but he had no clue what that meant. Comfort, closeness… intimacy? He groaned quietly and rolled over onto his stomach again, burying his face in the pillow that smelled like Cam.

Austin was too damn old to go through this crap.

Perhaps being on his own for a while was the answer. Support was good—that was one thing—but growing dependent on someone wasn't healthy. He couldn't count on Cam to save him, though he did want the man close. He had come to like this place, despite not having spent a lot of time here. But it was homey, not too big, and comfortable. Not as flashy as his own house across town. A house Jade had picked out and decorated.

Fucking Jade.

He had to talk to her. The more he thought about it, the more he suspected his wife of using Austin's current state as an excuse to get out. Had he missed something in the past? It wasn't that unlikely. They had, after all, had their issues.

Hour-by-hour, he reminded himself. Right. Hour-by-hour. He would deal with everything; he had to. *Gun or no gun.* No matter the consequences, obstacles, or reactions from others, he'd do it. Starting with breakfast with Cam.

Dragging himself out of bed, he reached for his borrowed sweatpants, went to the bathroom, took a leak and freshened up, then padded out to the kitchen. He winced a little at the lingering pain in his leg from last night's bar fight.

That was another thing… Austin had never been a fighter. But he'd seen red. He had punched that bastard over and over, getting a few in return, until the bouncer had broken it up.

Yeah, I'm a mess, all right.

Cam was standing by the stove, his back to Austin, and his

shoulders looked tense.

"Good morning," Austin said carefully. He was suddenly worried that Cam was the one who'd ended up regretting last night.

Cam nodded curtly. He didn't turn around.

Gun or no gun. Austin steeled himself and did what he *wanted*; he walked up to him, gently placing his hands on Cam's hips, and dropped a soft kiss on his shoulder.

Cam stopped what he was doing and hung his head. His shoulders slumped. In defeat or relief, Austin couldn't tell. He hoped for the latter, though.

"No fucking regrets?"

Austin shook his head slowly and kissed Cam's shoulder again, this time lingering. "I told you." Damn, it felt good to be this close to Cam. It was liberating. Giving Cam a nudge, he silently told him to turn around. Cam complied, and as soon as they faced each other, Austin tilted his head and got Cam's lips. "You thought I'd regret it," he murmured between brushing kisses.

"I thought you'd fuck this up," Cam corrected and slid his arms around Austin's midsection. "I thought shit would get weird, and then…" He trailed off, burying his face in the crook of Austin's neck, and kissed the spot behind his ear. "We know you can be an idiot sometimes."

Austin smirked. "An idiot who *you* broke that rule with."

"Oh, for fuck's sake." Cam groaned and shoved Austin away. "I knew that was gonna come back and bite me in the ass." He shook his head. "Now, get outta my sight. I'm making scrambled eggs. Bastard."

Austin laughed, relieved, and headed out to the patio where Bourbon was playing with a chew toy. Curious, he walked over to the pool and toed the plastic cover, appeased when he found it fairly solid. In other words, Bourbon could run all over it and not fall through any cracks.

A WHILE LATER, Austin and Cam sat on the patio and drank coffee and ate scrambled eggs. Both of which tasted a little burnt.

"Never claimed I was good at cooking," Cam said offhandedly.

"I'm not very picky." Austin took a sip of his coffee and looked out over the pool. "Any plans this weekend?"

"Nope. You?"

"Not really." Austin frowned to himself, thinking he should probably do *something.* He couldn't really handle sitting around doing nothing anymore. "I suppose I have some thinking to do."

Cam nodded pensively, eyes on his plate. "I'd be your shoulder to cry on, but that's usually your job." He sent Austin a forced smile.

"Yeah, because you've never comforted me," Austin said dryly. Christ, it felt like they were both in need of their mommas.

Gale kept commenting on how unorthodox it would be if Austin and Cam *didn't* need comfort, but it did little to change Austin's mind. Crying like a baby was for the weak. Not that anyone had ever told him that; it was just how he felt. Although, it only applied to himself, in his opinion. He didn't find Cam odd for being depressed or anxious. He understood it, and whenever Cam was down, Austin wanted to be there.

Once again, it reminded him of Gale's question about whether or not he felt like Cam was his responsibility, and he had finally come up with his answer. No, he didn't see Cam as a responsibility. Not at all. He was only protective.

Austin cared about him. A lot.

"Remember when I got sick?" Austin murmured after a while. Cam nodded with a dip of his chin. "You made sure I ate."

A WEEK LATER, at least they guessed it had been a week, the entire basement reeked more than it ever had. Pete's body was rotting in Chris's cell, and several of the guys were taking turns puking their guts out in the toilets.

Austin's stomach churned as he dropped to the floor next to the toilet. He was completely empty, weak, and on the verge of breaking down. Slick with cold sweat, he tried to regain his breath.

At this point, he could barely lift his arm to grab the cup of water next to him.

Mr. Cruel, as he now wanted to be called, was as unaffected as ever when he delivered meals and water. Too weak to get it himself, Austin let Cam grab their food. At least Cam had become a bit nicer since their fight last week.

"Eat." Cam sat down on the floor next to Austin and held up a bowl of soup and a spoon.

While Cam flushed the toilet, Austin forced himself up to a sitting position, rinsed his mouth with water and some toothpaste, then accepted the bowl. The chicken broth made him want to gag, but he needed the sustenance. Even more, he needed water. The only thing that held back his tears was that he needed to contain whatever fluids he had left in his system. Extreme survival instincts had kicked in, but that didn't mean his mind was strong enough to fend off the feeling of hopelessness.

No matter how long they waited, none of the men ever saw an opportunity to overpower their kidnapper and get back to freedom. Not even a couple days ago when another man—Victor—had been "called to an interview" upstairs.

Victor, named Fred by the madman, had the character of an older brother, and he had been pushed down the stairs after a beating. Cuffed behind his back. Gagged. Shot in the thigh. Numerous fractures. The man was in agony, but there was nothing anybody could do.

"Jesus." Cam leaned toward the toilet, not sure if he was about to throw up or not. But the man look nauseated, Austin could tell. "I could kill for fresh air and a couple cheeseburgers."

Austin groaned, his gut tightening. "Prime rib, man. Cold beer, some damn sunshine, baked potatoes, and a dip in the pool."

"Oh, yeah. Pizza."

"Fried chicken…"

"A fuckin' burrito."

"Tacos."

"We're masochists, Austin."

"Clearly."

The melancholy that fell over them was heavier than usual.

Austin had always been one of those who suffered in silence, but he didn't really see it as suffering. He never had high demands. As long as he had a roof over his head, some comfort, food on the table, and was able to keep his daughter happy, everything was all right. Sure, he'd been stuck in a rut with his wife for a few years now, but he didn't complain. You couldn't have everything in life. But in this moment, there were things Austin would actually take a life to have. Basic stuff, like fresh air, safety, good food, a shower—oh God, he wanted a shower. He wanted to soak in water for days. For the first time in his life, he wanted something so badly that it physically hurt.

Another thing that physically hurt was how much he missed his baby girl. No one could comfort Austin the way Riley could. And he craved that to the point of desperation—comfort. Closeness. The thought of a simple hug from Riley made him ache.

"Listen up!" boomed a voice from outside. "After you're done eating, it's time I have a little chat with Sam."

Austin's head snapped up, his wide eyes meeting Cam's equally wide ones.

Sam was the name of Austin's character.

"NOW WE CAN eat whatever we want, and we're suffering through this bullshit." Cam pushed away his plate. "I'm ordering a fucking pizza. You want?"

Austin was leaning his elbows on the table, his fingers massaging his temples. He shook his head no in answer, but that was all he could muster. It wasn't often flashbacks sucked him in like this one had; he could remember without feeling the need to vomit afterward. There were no anxiety attacks, just hatred toward that fucking bastard who had kidnapped them. But now... fuck. He felt raw and vulnerable.

Before he knew it, another flashback pulled him under.

"WAIT," CAM RUSHED in a whisper. He put his cuffed hands on Austin's shoulder and pulled him back from the door. "We should try."

"Try?" Austin arched a brow. "What are you talking about?"

Cam gave him an impatient look. "We'll try to defeat him. The two of us. Right now. Gun or no gun—we have to give it a go."

"Even if we're cuffed behind our backs?"

"Yes." Cam stepped closer and lowered his voice. "Ram into him. Shoulder him in the gut or something. I don't fucking know—pretend you're a football player. Tackle him. I'll follow right behind and try to take his gun."

It was too tempting to pass up, even if Austin was in serious pain and had just spent the past two days being sick. Perhaps they'd been here so long that they'd lost a pinch of fear for something that could end their lives in a heartbeat. The gun their kidnapper liked to wave around—and use, for that matter—wasn't as dangerous anymore.

"Okay." Austin took a breath and nodded. "Okay."

The two men steeled themselves and stood shoulder to shoulder, waiting as the unsuspecting devil outside opened the hatch.

"Uncuff yourselves."

Austin and Cam knew the procedure. They got rid of their restraints only to put them back on, this time behind their backs, and lastly threw out the keys again. Then the door started to slide open, and Austin exchanged a quick look with Cam.

"Gun or no gun," Cam mouthed.

It would be their motto in the future.

Austin nodded minutely—gun or no gun—and flexed his muscles. With a final, deep breath, he faced the opening and charged forward just as the man raised his gun.

Forcefully slamming into their kidnapper, Austin caught him totally off guard, and he almost dropped his gun. Almost. They tumbled to the dirty floor, Austin landing on top. Despite his arms burning and his inability to use them, Austin struggled like a savage. He spat out a curse and brought his knee up to the other man's chest. But just as he heard Cam scrambling over to them, a shot was fired.

"Motherfucker!" Cam screamed.

Without thinking, Austin turned his head in Cam's direction, and his face paled when he saw that he'd been shot. Cam—damn it, Cam had been hit. In the shoulder. Shoulder; quick thinking. You could survive a bullet in the shoulder, and with that conclusion, Austin turned back to wrestle his way to victory. But it was too late. That tiny second Austin had spent checking on Cam was all the madman needed to regain leverage.

Instead of glaring into brown, beady eyes, Austin was staring into the barrel of a gun.

"Get. Off. Me," the crazy man growled.

"CAM," AUSTIN CHOKED out and doubled over in his seat. He gasped repeatedly, trying to get air into his lungs. In the background, he could hear Cam speaking urgently to him, but he couldn't for the life of him hear what he was saying. All he could see, hear, and feel belonged in that metal cage. The smell of death and despair, every ache and sorrow, all that anger and desperation…

If a man was shot, you reacted. You called 911, you tried to help, you prioritized that person. But Austin and Cam had been driven to the point where perfect health didn't matter. Broken bones, bruises, and bloodshed… it was all *nothing*—as long as they could get out alive. And it sounded plausible in theory, but to actually sink that low, where that way of thinking became natural, where men became savages… was it weird that only Cam could understand Austin? Was it so damn weird that he couldn't connect with Jade?

He was still part savage. He was still struggling to get back to being human. *Treat a person like an animal, and he'll become one.* But like Cam, Austin was decent at faking. Not great, but decent. When in reality, he just wanted to crawl into a hole and fall apart.

"Austin!"

He could feel Cam's hands on him, his cheeks, his forehead, yet focus remained out of reach. He was dizzy, nauseated, and out of breath. His lungs burned.

"Snap out of it. Talk to me, baby." Someone was shaking him, holding him. "Austin! Come on!"

SOONER RATHER THAN *later, Austin ended up in the room on the first floor that Cam had described to him. But he wasn't directed to sit at the table like Cam had been. Instead he found himself attached to a chain that was fastened to a hook in the ceiling. Both feet were still firmly on the ground and his cuffed hands remained behind his back, but Austin had no room to move whatsoever.*

The two-inch thick chain was like a choking snake around his body. It circled his legs, his midsection, his chest, his arms, and his damn neck. His skin got pinched between the links if he even tried to move, and if he so much as tilted his head, it was like breathing through a straw.

"You used to be my friend, Sam."

Austin groaned in pain, trying to focus. "My—my name is Austin," he panted. Christ, the links were really digging in everywhere, and his arms were twisted, the chain pulling too tightly. "It's Austin Huntley. Not Sam."

"Silence!" The scream was piercing. "Now—" a deep breath "—as I was saying. You used to be my friend, Sam." The man approached slowly, and there was a knife in his hand. "Then you became the king of baseball and forgot about me. You made my senior year hell, and you have no idea how hard I fought to make sure my family believed I was still a star." He spat in Austin's face. "You ignored me in the halls, you laughed when Kirk and the others pulled pranks on me, and you—"

"I'm not Sam, you sick bastard!"

For that, Austin earned himself a fist in the gut, and it was only the beginning. He was beaten over every inch of his body. The knife sliced through his skin in several places—deeply, but superficially enough to keep him alive.

It was torture. Literally.

Blood trickled down Austin's arms, jaw, legs, and hairline.

He screamed out, white-hot pain spreading through him in radiating waves, when his arms were twisted and yanked up farther, dislocating his left shoulder.

Next, his other shoulder was pulled out of its socket, too.

"You—you—" Austin coughed and spluttered; he'd bitten his tongue, so blood slowly filled his mouth with a coppery flavor "—goddamn c-coward!" He glared at the shorter man. "You won't fight fair; you w-won't *even show your face."*

Austin really needed to stop goading him.

Then again, if you thought you were about to die, you wanted some pride restored before you went, right? And Austin did believe this was it for him. His thoughts were filled with memories, the moments in his life he cherished the most. The day his daughter was born, the day he graduated from graduate school and his parents were beaming with pride, the moment Jade announced she was pregnant...

"I will kill you last, Sam. You know why? Because I want to draw it out. Betrayal is the biggest crime, in my opinion."

ELEVEN

To Cam, it felt like forever before Austin came around. And if this was how Cam acted during an anxiety attack, he couldn't understand how his family—Austin included—handled it. 'Cause seeing Austin so distressed and completely out of it was fucking painful.

He wondered how aware Austin was of his surroundings—if he knew they were on the patio floor. It was when Austin had nearly fallen over that Cam had guided them both down here. Now he was leaning against the back wall of the house, and he had Austin half-lying in front of him, his head on Cam's naked chest. Over and over, Cam murmured words of no significance to Austin, hoping he was listening. They weren't back in hell. They were here. Safe. Together. No one was gonna torture them.

Cam wasn't sure if he admired Austin or if he was frustrated with him. Even in the middle of panic and anxiety, the man broke down in silence. He was crying, but he didn't make a sound. His breaths were shallow and rapid, but there was no plea for help.

"You're safe," he whispered and kissed the top of Austin's head. Reaching down, he threaded their fingers together. "If you hear me, can you please give my hand a squeeze or something?" He needed Austin to be all right, for fuck's sake. *Now.* He had no patience.

It also infuriated him to think that Austin's wife was a goddamn bitch who wouldn't help. Not that Cam was sure he wanted that, but technically... she should. Yeah, Cam liked the feeling of being helpful—especially with this man—and there was an odd sense of satisfaction from being the one to whom Austin turned. But he hated that Austin didn't have any other options.

"Thank Christ," Cam mumbled when Austin gave his hand a weak squeeze. Tears continued to soak Cam's chest, but at this point, he was just relieved. Austin evidently needed this, and Cam was determined to be the strong one this time. "I'm here," he murmured, slightly uncomfortable. Not with Austin, per se, but displays of affection weren't Cam's forte. He wanted strict directions on how to help; now he was doing this blindly, not knowing what worked.

"S-sorry," Austin croaked minutes later.

Cam rolled his eyes, as he didn't see the big deal. There was no reason to apologize. "Shut the fuck up and cry or whatever." He winced, regretting his wording. "I meant what I said." He cleared his throat. "I'm here—for you. And, um, you don't have to be so fucking strong all the time." Okay. He exhaled. That was a little better. He hoped. Then he remembered the shrink's words about letting it all out—it was healthy and shit. And Austin had made Cam do that, too. "You're supposed to talk about it," he said quietly. "What were you remembering?" Austin let out a shuddering breath and began to sit up, but Cam didn't let go. "Fuck that. Stay here." He wrapped his arms around Austin's shoulders. "If not for you, then for me."

Austin seemed relieved as he melted into Cam's arms. He was clearly not used to leaning on others—physically or metaphorically. He didn't ask for help—goddamn masochist. Then again, was Cam any better? Hell, no.

What a fucking pair they made.

"You got shot…" Austin mumbled, which was all he needed to say for Cam to be clued in on what period of time in captivity he was stuck in. "We were so damn helpless."

Cam pressed down his own anxiety and focused on Austin. That time in the cell had been one of the worst, and Austin was right: they'd been helpless. There had been nothing to do to prevent torture and death. All because of one raging lunatic.

CAM HISSED IN pain as he finally managed to reach his cot. It had taken a solid hour for him to drag himself a few feet and then pull himself up to the cot. His shoulder was burning, a warm trickle of blood steadily oozing out of the front. Only one trickle, which meant there was no exit wound. The bullet was still lodged inside him.

His eyes stung with sweat and silent tears, and he wished he could at least get rid of the motherfucking handcuffs. But his misery aside, he was also worried about Austin. After the shit they had pulled, he had a feeling Psycho wasn't gonna go easy on Austin.

"You okay, man?" Chase asked.

"Fuckin' peachy," Cam groaned. Everyone already knew what had happened, but a failed attempt at escaping was quickly becoming old news.

Before long, it was Austin's turn to tumble down the uneven stairs, and Cam held his breath, for unknown reasons visibly upset at the thought of his cellmate being tortured. Annoyed, Cam tried to blink back his tears, but they kept rolling down his cheeks. Fucking pussy. He hated showing weakness.

First, the hatch opened, and Psycho peered inside, spotting Cam on the cot. Then the door was pushed open, and Psycho himself dragged Austin's body inside. He dropped two keys and a larger medical kit on the floor, said, "Patch each other up. I'm not ready for either of you to quit the company yet," and then left.

AN IRON FIST squeezed Cam's heart as he remembered Austin's lifeless body.

He guessed it was the fact that a single man had caused so much pain to ten strong men that made them angry these days. It wasn't necessarily pride that got wounded; it was disbelief that made him rage. Regardless of the prison-like setting, the handcuffs, the guns, the mind games, and the torture, it was difficult to believe that one man could have so much control.

It seemed to have hit Austin the hardest. The man always needed to be useful, and for some reason he couldn't see that without him, Cam would definitely be dead. Austin failed to realize just how much he'd helped Cam.

He let out a labored breath and nuzzled Austin's hair. "You always patched me up. Don't forget that." Not to mention the countless times he'd helped Cam with his anxiety attacks.

"You kept me alive," Austin rasped. "I was too weak."

"You—*Christ*, Austin. You weren't weak." Cam pushed down his temper. "Do you even remember how bruised you were?"

Cam sure as fuck did.

TAKING OFF THE cuffs was priority number one. Then Cam had woken Austin by splashing water in his face, and Austin had been conscious long enough to croak out where it hurt the most. And, uh, well, it had taken Cam seven tries to put Austin's shoulders back in their sockets. He felt bad, but he wasn't a fucking doctor.

Anyway, Austin had passed out from the pain, and that brought them to now. Cam was tending to the knife wounds after having stripped Austin of clothes—one pair of shredded sweatpants and one filthy T-shirt. And when he was done with Austin's face, he had to cut up both their T-shirts, 'cause there weren't enough bandages in the medical kit for both of them.

Four wounds needed stitches, so Cam was glad Austin was still passed out on the floor. Without anesthesia or even the weakest painkiller, it was bound to hurt like a bitch. But the most important thing was to close the cuts and make sure everything was as clean as possible. The alcohol he poured probably stung like hell, too.

He made sure to save some for himself, 'cause when Austin was ready, he was gonna have to dig out the bullet in Cam's shoulder.

"What the fuck did he do to you?" Cam whispered, not expecting an answer. He gently swiped a cotton ball soaked in alcohol over the four-inch long cut along Austin's temple, right at his hairline. Butterfly bandages should suffice there.

He noticed that Austin was coming around when he whimpered and a stray tear slid down his temple.

"You're gonna be okay."

"Hurts," Austin choked out, eyes closed.

"I know," Cam murmured thickly. "Can you tell me if anything is broken?"

"I... um. I d-don't know..."

Cam nodded to himself and resumed his work. With Austin wearing only his black boxer briefs, Cam could see every bit of damage, and Jesus fucking Christ, there was a lot. For the wounds along the man's thighs and calves, he pressed sterile pads directly onto the cuts, and then he tore cotton strips off of the T-shirts to create bandages to tie around Austin's legs.

While Cam tended to Austin's arms, Psycho returned, but before panic could settle in, the men found out he was only down there to "fetch the dead guy." Pete. A rotting corpse. Pete, an innocent man. Whom Psycho had called Dad. Fucking lunatic.

"I need you to wake the fuck up now, Austin," Cam stated. He didn't understand it, but seeing Austin this way was just wrong. This was the man who'd helped him when Cam was nothing but an asshole. Yeah, so he needed to wake up and be good again. "There's nothing more I can do." He surveyed Austin's body. "I cleaned up the blood, I stitched you up, I-I don't think, um... I mean, I don't think there's a big risk of infection. How're your fucking shoulders?"

Austin let out a quiet, pained moan, but that was about it.

"Well, at least you're breathing," Cam muttered, then winced when he accidentally moved his bad shoulder. "Goddamn, I could use a drink."

EYES STINGING WITH unshed tears, Cam tightened his hold on Austin. He shuddered. His hands slid over Austin's exposed skin, encountering too many scars. Some were fading. Some were too deep to ever go away.

In the pocket of his shorts, his phone vibrated, but he ignored it. Before Austin had woken up this morning, someone had been calling Cam's phone multiple times from an unknown number, and he didn't respond to that shit.

"Are you with me, Austin?" Cam murmured. He hoped he wouldn't get freaked out whenever Austin grew quiet now.

"Yeah…"

Cam let out a soft breath. "Come on. Let's go inside instead." The sun was at its highest. Even Bourbon had retreated to the shadows on the other side of the pool where he was gnawing on a bone. The high, wooden fence that surrounded the backyard provided seclusion, but unless you were in that pool, it was like a broiling pan in the middle of the day. "We'll talk and rest for a bit, and then we're ordering that pizza." He was gonna make sure Austin pulled through this.

To do that, he swallowed his aversion to his medicine and took a damn pill that made it easier to prevent anxiety attacks.

AUSTIN WASN'T TIRED; he was utterly drained. It felt like he'd been crying for days and not a couple hours. His voice was hoarse and shook when he spoke. His eyes felt heavy. But Cam kept pushing. Gently. Persistently. He made sure Austin talked about what he was remembering.

"No—open your eyes." Cam kissed him between his eyebrows. "If anything, I need to hear what came next, 'cause I don't fucking remember."

"You were pretty out of it," Austin mumbled sleepily and pulled the blanket up higher. Before, when they'd made it to bed, Cam had switched on the ceiling fan as well as a table fan that stood on the low wall behind Cam's back. So, the living room was now comfortably cool even though the sun was scorching right outside.

"Keep talking," Cam said, just a hint of irritation in his voice.

Austin's eyes remained closed, but he managed a smile. Cam wouldn't be Cam if he didn't get annoyed.

"Nothing much to tell," Austin lied as the memories flooded back.

"BITE DOWN ON this." Austin placed a few strips of fabric that he'd twisted together between Cam's teeth. They were both on the floor, Cam's head in Austin's lap, and it was time to take out that damn bullet. Well, Cam insisted it was. Austin was torn.

Austin couldn't describe his own pain; it was too great, too consuming. He was dizzy with it, and he was fighting against infection. Nevertheless, it had been almost a day now, and Cam was getting worse.

A fever meant that your body was struggling—working to beat a virus... or some foreign object that simply didn't belong in a man's shoulder. It meant your immune system was functioning. But there was no way of knowing whether you'd be able to win or lose. In Cam's case, Austin was worried. Not because he had a fever, but because he complained over the cold—when in reality, it was still humid and hot down here. Cam's teeth were chattering, which meant there was a long way to go.

Austin remembered one time Riley had been down with the flu. After a couple days, she'd begun to sweat profusely, and she had hated *it—said it was icky and gross. But Austin's mother had explained to her it was a good thing: Riley's little body had beat the infection, and she'd be back to normal in no time.*

Unless Cam's fever went down soon, there was a big risk his body would cave from fatigue and shut down. Though, this was only if there was, in fact, an infection. For all Austin knew, Cam's fever could be caused by the bullet wound itself.

"You sure about this?" Austin asked for the hundredth time as he pulled out a pair of pad-tipped tweezers. "If there's nerve damage or an artery's been hit, there's nothing I can do once the bullet is out." He'd watched enough TV to know that much. "Cam—" he cupped his cheek, forcing him to look Austin in the eye "—do you understand what I'm saying? You can bleed to death."

"My fucking choice," Cam gritted out, the sound muffled by the strip of rope between his teeth. "Get that damn bullet outta me."

Sighing heavily, Austin removed the temporary dressing Cam had applied yesterday. It didn't bleed too much, and he was glad to see there was neither discoloration nor too much swelling.

"On the count of three," he mumbled, but as he said *"one"* and listened as Cam released a breath, he gently slid the tweezers inside the wound.

Cam cried out through clenched teeth that clamped down harshly on the fabric in his mouth. Every muscle in his body tensed up. But Austin kept going. Holding Cam still, he continued until the rounded tips of the tool came in contact with something metallic. It was a silent little snick that Austin merely felt through the tweezers.

"Almost, buddy." Austin's brow furrowed in concentration, and he managed to pinch the bullet on his second try. A few beads of sweat trickled down his temples; meanwhile, Cam was shaking and his face was pale.

It was a miracle Cam hadn't gone into shock yesterday, but now Austin feared it was happening right this moment. Smoothly removing the bullet, Austin dropped it on the floor and immediately started to clean up. He spared no alcohol, and he used plenty of antiseptic cream before he sealed the wound with sterile pads and medical tape.

"It's done, Cam," he whispered and removed the makeshift rope from Cam's mouth. *"It's all done."* The only response he got was a weak nod as Cam's eyes fluttered closed. *"No, stay with me."* Austin carefully pulled him over to the blanket he'd rolled together earlier to form a long pillow. Because he'd feared this. Austin had feared Cam would either go into shock or bleed out. And if any of that was going to happen, Austin needed to stay close. *"Can you open your eyes?"* He made sure Cam didn't put any pressure on his shoulder.

They both lay down on the hard floor, but it was at least warmer than the cots, and Cam needed heat. It was survival instinct that kicked in again, so Austin unceremoniously drew the second blanket over them and scooted close enough for their bodies to touch.

"Look at me." Austin palmed Cam's cheek and gently brushed away

some moisture under his eyes. And at last, Cam forced his eyes to open, causing Austin to breathe out in relief. "You're going to be okay. You're not bleeding a lot at all, okay? That's good news."

"F-fuc-ckin' c-cold," Cam exhaled, his teeth still chattering.

Austin nodded and moved even closer. "We'll get that temperature up in no time, I promise." Truth be told, he knew little to nothing about this. He'd gone hiking a lot with his dad when he was younger, so he knew a thing or two about patching up a wound, but nothing serious. Treating a shock victim... that was for doctors, for Christ's sake.

Wanting Cam to get warmer as quickly as possible, Austin tucked Cam's head under his chin and held him close to his body. In turn, Cam burrowed into Austin's heat and tried to get his muscles to relax. Maybe it was shock; maybe it wasn't. It could be the fever, but it didn't really matter when both things required warmth.

Both men were in an indescribable amount of pain, but exhaustion won in the end, and they fell asleep.

"YOU WERE SO goddamn stubborn about that bullet," Austin croaked.

He blinked back tears, thinking about what-ifs, which was never a good thing. It was the main reason he couldn't be honest with his parents. Maggie had already lost one son, and every time she saw Austin now, she drove herself to tears with what could've happened. Therefore, he acted as if life was good—or at least better. Good enough.

"I didn't bleed out," Cam reminded him. "It worked."

"But what if—"

"Stop." Cam grabbed Austin's jaw and planted a firm kiss on his lips. "Don't think like that." His voice softened, and there was a small smirk in place. "You'll give yourself more grays."

"Piss off." Austin's head dropped to the pillow again, and he ran a hand over his hair—*with very few grays in it.* "You could let me sleep instead. I'm so fucking tired."

Cam tsked. "Such language for Mr. MBA." His smile touched Austin's forehead. "I distinctly remember a time where you wouldn't let *me* sleep."

Oh, Austin remembered, too. He'd never forget. But at least this memory was on the lighter side.

"DRINK SOME MORE, but do it slowly." Austin held up the tin cup of water to Cam's mouth.

Perhaps a few would think it was an act of kindness when their captor—no, screw that; he was a damn torturer—delivered food to them without demanding they put on their cuffs first. But Austin and Cam didn't think he had a kind bone in him. He wanted his victims to suffer, which they definitely were, and Austin supposed the asshole also knew what the men could handle. Right now, for instance, it would be nearly impossible to get around if they couldn't use their hands. So, this was the second day Austin and Cam had received food and water, yet they were allowed to keep what was left of the medical kit, and they didn't have to restrain themselves.

Cam was recovering at a snail's pace, but at least he could sit up—with help. He was weak, and the fever was still there, though he was more alert.

"*I wanna sleep,*" *Cam grumbled.*

"*Not yet.*" *Austin, who was leaning back against the wall near the toilet—convenience and all—had Cam in front of him, seated on the floor between his legs. It offered Cam more heat, and his back to Austin's chest was a hell of a lot more comfortable than the floor. It had been months of sleeping on hard surfaces; their bodies ached in protest whenever they moved.*

"*I feel bad for your wife.*" *Cam was bitching again.* "*You're a fuckin' doctor nazi—lemme sleep.*"

"*She doesn't act like a child when she's sick,*" *Austin said, but instead of getting annoyed at Cam, there was a small smile in his voice. He was getting used to Cam's behavior.* "*Come on.*" *He peered over Cam's shoulder and brought the cup closer to his lips.* "*Drink, buddy.*"

"*And then you'll shut up and let me sleep?*"

Austin chuckled. "*Yes. I'll shut up and let you sleep.*"

"*Jesus Christ. Fine,*" *Cam muttered. Between a couple slow sips of water, he said,* "*A good nurse would at least offer a sponge bath.*"

"*You called me a doctor nazi first. Doctors don't give sponge baths.*"

Cam huffed and took another sip of water. "*Nazi Nurse—that's your new name.*"

"*You'd use me like that, huh?*" *Austin cracked a grin as he gently dragged the washcloth over Cam's neck and good shoulder.* "*While I'd be working my skills, you'd fantasize about supermodels.*"

Cam hummed quietly, neither confirming nor denying.

"YOU WERE A fucking hard-ass," Cam chuckled. "Consider this payback."

"I eventually did let you sleep," Austin pointed out.

"You never gave me a sponge bath."

Austin couldn't help but laugh. "At least now I know you probably wouldn't fantasize about supermodels." It felt good to laugh, even if he was tired. While he hated to depend on somebody else, it left him more refreshed. Maybe he'd needed this. It was just so damn liberating.

"Hmmm. No. I can think something better than skinny women." Cam ran his hand down Austin's back. "Ever thought about wearing heels?"

Austin huffed. "That's not even a little funny." He opened his eyes to see Cam failing at hiding his amusement. "Come here," he murmured, leaning in for a kiss.

It started light, but Cam had a way of evoking feelings Austin had only thought he was familiar with.

His entire body buzzed with a harsh need to claim.

Ending up on top of Cam, he pushed aside his tiredness for something much more satisfactory. He kissed Cam deeply, the two exploring each other's mouths.

Austin wasn't sure if he was supposed to be wary of anything. All he knew was that it felt freeing to be with Cam. They grabbed at each other roughly, both fairly dominant, but that didn't mean Austin was shunning the idea of submitting. He hoped that applied to Cam, too. Because the closer they were, the better it felt. There was no thought about semantics or details—as long as he could ravish and be ravished in return.

"Christ, you're sexy," he muttered as the thought hit him. But it was true. Cam was a fucking vision. So different from what he was used to, yet appealing all the same. Austin was drawn to Cam's masculinity—his swimmer's body, his strength, his damn voice, and his rough-around-the-edges personality.

Austin could let himself be comforted by all that hardness. But at the same time, he was equally attracted to Cam's softer sides. The vulnerability he tried so hard to hide, the insecurities, and the sometimes-awkward fumblings with words. Those were the traits that brought out Austin's inner caveman, for reasons unknown to him.

Feeling Cam's hard cock grinding against his own, he pushed his hips forward and moaned into their sloppy kiss. "I want you." Understatement. He'd wanted more last night, too, but he was slightly self-conscious about the fact that he'd never been with a guy before. He wanted it to be good for Cam, so he'd chickened out when it came to oral sex. But now… "Stand up." Breathing heavily, he rolled away and pointed to the space between the bed and the coffee table.

"I thought you were tired." Cam's voice was thick with lust as he gave Austin a final kiss before complying. In answer, Austin just shook his head—half a lie. He was tired, but not enough to shake off the desire to taste Cam. "Now what?" Cam cocked a brow once he was standing, his hands on his hips, and he was watching Austin with a small dare in his eyes.

Austin just smirked to himself and scooted to the edge of the bed. His feet hit the hardwood floor, one on either side of Cam, and he leaned forward to kiss his thigh. As Cam sucked in a breath, Austin hooked his fingers underneath the waistbands of shorts and boxers, tugged both down Cam's legs, and exposed him fully.

"You don't have to—" Cam started to say in a rush, but he stopped himself and ran a hand through his hair. "Fuck that. Only an idiot would say no, and I've pictured this too many times. Keep going."

Austin chuckled under his breath and nuzzled the soft skin of Cam's hip. Slowly, he slid his hands up Cam's thighs, refusing to get nervous. A guy didn't find a blow job bad. There were good ones, great ones, and goddamn glorious ones. Austin knew what he wanted for himself. Not too much teasing—that was just irritating. A lot of suction, wetness, and his balls massaged. He could do that.

Right?

Austin hummed, turned on by the musky scent of Cam's arousal. He was hard, uncut, long, not too thick, and the area around was smoother than he expected. Austin trimmed sometimes, but it wasn't a habit.

Kissing the root of Cam's cock, he gripped the length of it and stroked slowly but firmly. At the same time, he licked his lips and began to kiss his way to the head. *Jesus Christ.* He got into it. More than he thought he would. With his lips wrapped around Cam, he took him as deep as he could.

"Fuckin'... oh, *fuck.*" Cam trembled with a shudder and wove his fingers through Austin's hair. "That's it—oh, yeah."

Austin closed his eyes and swirled his tongue around the swollen tip, and when he suckled it, he got the first taste of Cam's pre-come. It was salty and smooth on his tongue.

He wasn't crazy about the taste, but it did excite him more

than he could've imagined.

He groaned and took another inch, a bit more than he could really handle, but that didn't stop him. He sucked hard and made sure to use his tongue a lot. In return, Cam moaned and cursed.

After a few minutes, he began to fuck Austin's mouth, though he did so with caution. Which Austin didn't like. Moving his free hand to Cam's ass, he silently told him to let go. At least a bit more. Then Austin moved to stick that same hand down his own pants and stroked himself at the same pace he sucked Cam.

With each thrust of Cam's hips, Austin grew more confident. He cupped Cam's balls and tugged when he did the same to himself. He suckled the head of Cam's dick when he smeared a bead of pre-come over his own cock with his thumb. It was one of the most erotic things he'd ever done, including the early years in his marriage when Jade had been more adventurous.

"Oh, Christ," Cam moaned. "Are you jacking—shit, take off your pants. I wanna see you."

Austin backed away enough to push down his sweats and free his cock. He fisted it and stroked it hard, at the same time returning to Cam's dick which glistened with saliva and arousal. He sucked him in, moaning at how *fucking* turned on he was, and he only had one goal. To swallow Cam down.

In shallow thrusts, Cam fucked his mouth. "Holy fuck, Austin." He gritted his teeth. "Almost there." It was a warning—a chance for Austin to back away. "Make me come—*please.*"

That *please* went straight to Austin's cock, and he suddenly changed his mind about instant gratification. Breathing heavily, he pulled away as a rush of dominance settled in him.

Control.

"Lie down," he commanded quietly. "Now." His muscles tensed, and he watched Cam hungrily, who obeyed with a look of confusion. But Cam was at that point where he'd do anything to get off. Every man on the planet reached that point.

"Don't fucking tease me," Cam said, lying down on his back. He put one hand behind his head, the other one absently trailing up and down his chest. "Get over here."

Austin chuckled darkly and wiped his mouth. "Let's get one thing straight." He moved in between Cam's legs and hovered over him. "When I'm the one making you come, you're in no position to order me around." He nipped at Cam's bottom lip. "Am I making myself clear, baby?"

"Fuck," Cam breathed out, shivering violently. He swallowed and tilted his head for a kiss, but Austin moved just out of reach. "Yeah—fuck. Yes. Okay."

"Excellent." Austin stole a quick kiss, then settled back on his heels. As he stroked his cock, he dragged it teasingly along the crack of Cam's ass. "Why should I let you come?"

"'Cause you can't help yourself," Cam panted. Christ, he was desperate for Austin to touch him. It was easy to tell. "You want to." At Austin's arched brow, which meant business, Cam backtracked. "Fucking hell, Austin. I'll beg—is that what you want? I'll do anything; just… *get me off.*"

A slow smile spread on Austin's lips. "You probably shouldn't have said you'd do anything." At that, he pressed the tip of his cock against Cam's hole. "One might take advantage." He was teasing.

Mostly.

Cam let out a mix between a moan and a whimper and fisted his cock, stroking it roughly. "You wanna fuck me?" He jerked his chin at the coffee table. "There's a condom and lube in my wallet. But—" he sat up abruptly and grabbed Austin's jaw "—you better give up that sweet ass of yours one day, too." Cam was momentarily in charge. Austin was stunned, but his eyes betrayed the primal desire to be inside Cam. "You have no idea how many times I've wanted to bend you over and fuck you into next week. Am *I* making myself clear?"

Austin shuddered and nodded slowly, still processing. He closed his eyes. It was an odd feeling to both take and be taken. In these past twelve hours or so, he'd been swept off his fucking feet.

That he had to have Cam in his life had been established a long time ago, but now he was realizing just how much they'd grown to need each other—in every aspect. This wasn't a fluke or a way to pass time.

He didn't know how to explain himself to Cam, though. The emotions were all jumbled. Once upon a time, Jade had called him a romantic, but she'd gotten it all wrong. He could buy flowers, remember anniversaries, and dine her properly, but words failed him.

So, he just murmured, "I don't take this lightly." Then he kissed Cam, changing the tension from serious to heated in a second. "I want you to trust me on that."

Cam released a breath and lay down again. "Okay."

Reaching over to the coffee table, Austin retrieved a condom and a small packet of lube, one of those for one-time use. His focus was solely on Cam. He kissed his chest, stroked his cock, and settled between his legs once more. At least he'd had anal sex before. Even if it was more than ten years ago. And with a woman.

"Anything in particular you want before?" he asked as he nuzzled the base of Cam's cock. It had softened a little earlier, but now it was tight and hard again.

"Fingers," Cam grunted, bucking upward. "And suck my dick. Please."

He smiled and guided Cam's cock into his mouth, sucking strongly and wetly.

Just fingers for warm-up, though?

Give me some credit.

Austin had other plans. His right hand took over and stroked Cam; meanwhile, his mouth left a trail of open-mouthed kisses down to Cam's balls and farther down. He licked and sucked at the sensitive skin. More than once, he caught himself inhaling deeply. Mixed with arousal and fresh perspiration was also the scent of Cam's bodywash—the one Austin had borrowed last night in the shower.

The second Austin swiped his tongue over Cam's tight hole, Cam nearly arched off the bed. The curse he spat out was stuttered and gritty, and Austin literally felt how Cam's cock reacted. It strained in his moving hand. He'd definitely received his answer as to whether or not Cam liked having his ass tongue-fucked.

"*Jesus*, Austin!" Cam almost sounded annoyed—and very out of breath. He lifted himself up to support himself on his elbows.

"Warn a guy, will ya—oh, *God.*" Austin's only response was to close his lips over the light, smooth protrusion and apply pressure with his tongue. Cam's moans spurred him on. "Fuck, fuck, fuck…" The fucks trailed off into shallow breaths.

As if Austin needed more encouragement, Cam pulled up his knees, spread them farther apart, feet still planted on the mattress, and watched with hunger in his eyes. Those expressive eyes, silvery gray, darkened with lust into the color of liquid mercury. Austin held the gaze as he penetrated Cam's ass with his tongue, loosening the tight ring of muscle. For one moment, Cam threw his head back, and Austin was certain he'd never seen anything so goddamn sexy. At the same time, Austin felt a hot trickle of arousal seeping out of Cam's cock.

"You're driving me—" Cam gasped "—driving me insane."

When Austin deemed him ready, he replaced his tongue with his middle finger. A second finger was added within a couple minutes, and then a third. Every now and then, he'd pause to fuck him with his tongue and get him nice and wet.

He'd reduced Cam into a man who pleaded and whimpered instead of grunted and spat out curses.

"Fuck me, Austin," he panted. "I'm fucking begging you."

Both beyond ready, Austin pushed himself up and sat back to roll the condom down his cock. Next he tore off a corner on the packet of lube and coated two fingers that he brought to Cam's ass. He smeared the gleaming liquid around the hole, then pushed inside, only to repeat two, three times with more lube. With his free hand, he added the last of it to his cock. All slicked up and ready, he spent a minute or two rubbing Cam's prostate—just because Cam was so insanely sexy when he lost control. He was writhing and panting, sweat glistening on his torso, and his cock throbbed off of his abdomen.

Removing his fingers from Cam's ass, Austin wiped them on the sheet and gripped the base of his cock, dragging the tip teasingly around Cam's entrance. His heart was racing, and as much as he wasn't quite ready to delve deeper into whatever he felt for Cam, it was impossible not to acknowledge the significance. He moved higher up so they were face-to-face, and as he slowly began to push his cock inside, he dropped his forehead to Cam's, their labored breaths mingling in the small space between their parted lips.

"Yeah," Cam gritted out in a rush. "More."

Austin looked down between them, watching as his thick erection disappeared into Cam's tight ass. He groaned through clenched teeth and squeezed his eyes shut, countless sensations nearly bowling him over, but opened them again because he needed to see this. The feeling was… out of this fucking world. Tight, slick, hot. Just right.

Oh, holy mother of…

"Are you all right?" Austin asked huskily when he was all in.

"Uh-huh." Cam nodded jerkily and moved his hands to Austin's ass. There was both pain and pleasure reflected in his eyes. "Just been a while."

For the next several moments, Austin kissed and touched Cam wherever he could reach. He didn't start to move until Cam was begging him to, and then all bets were off. They were both attentive, but that didn't mean slow or gentle. They let go. Driven by desire and need, they unconsciously unleashed the savage mind-sets they'd had in captivity.

With each thrust of Austin's cock, Cam pushed back and urged him on.

"Don't fucking stop." Cam dug his heels into Austin's ass and pulled him in for a bruising kiss. "Don't stop, don't stop."

"I won't." Austin moved a hand down between them to stroke Cam. "I can't." The slide of his cock inside Cam's ass was addictive; it was impossible to stop. "I need this—you." He slid out then slammed back in, causing two loud moans to mingle with the sloppy kiss. "I need you." He massaged Cam's tongue with his own, teeth grazing and nipping. And inside of him... it was like a storm building up. Indescribable emotions raged and surged, leaving him raw and open.

A fuck couldn't alter a man's feelings, but perhaps it could make him realize things.

As far as Austin knew, lust came first, but that wasn't true here. Somewhere in the past six months, he'd started to fall for Cam, and now there was no going back. He'd been blindsided by terms like friendship and brotherhood, maybe even brothers-in-arms, but this went deeper.

He didn't have a lot to compare with, but he knew several things for certain. It wasn't his wife's words of comfort he sought. It wasn't his own house he wanted to spend time in anymore. It wasn't Jade's body he wanted to explore, be near, and fucking ravish.

Peering down at Cam's sculpted body, he knew no trauma could cause this kind of attraction. He could've understood wanting Cam as a security blanket after everything they'd been through, but that wasn't it.

Austin fucked the man under him harder and faster, not because it provided comfort, but because he fucking loved him.

He didn't know if he'd fallen completely; he didn't feel like reading into it anyway, but he finally knew where he was headed— where *this* was headed.

"Let me make you come." He kissed Cam 'til they were both breathless. Austin was on the brink of orgasm, too. "*Christ.*" He sucked on Cam's bottom lip as his balls drew up and tightened, as the familiar tingling sensation traveled down his spine, and as he buried his cock deep in Cam's ass over and over and over.

"Close," Cam gritted out. "Oh fuck, Austin!" He dug his head back into the pillow, his back arching. "You gotta come, too. *Now.*"

Like Austin had a choice. He'd already lost his struggle. Rocking deeper into Cam's ass, his climax took over just as the first rope of come pulsed out of Cam's cock. Austin's thighs throbbed, one with a twinge of pain, but he didn't stop. Through shudders and panting moans, they rode out their orgasms.

Austin rubbed Cam's soaked dick and inhaled deeply, feeling his mouth water. It was heady and nearly dizzying.

As the last trickles of their releases seeped out of their cocks, Austin brought a wet finger to Cam's mouth and brushed it over his lips. And just as the tip of Cam's tongue slipped out, Austin was there to kiss and lick it all up. Their tongues met passionately, tasting the salty arousal, tasting each other.

The kiss eventually slowed, and they floated in a comfortable silence with words left unsaid. They could both feel it, see it, as they looked at each other. The green in Austin's hazel eyes shone brighter than the brown, and the darkness in Cam's silvery eyes had faded.

Austin expected it and wasn't surprised when Cam averted his eyes, knowing that eye contact wasn't always easy for Cam. So, Austin brushed a final kiss between Cam's brows and slowly slid out his softening cock.

"Let's clean up, Mr. MBA," Cam said quietly. "Then you're gonna sleep."

TWELVE

AUSTIN TWISTED AND turned in his sleep. It was just his naked body under the blanket, but his mind went back to a time where a specific pair of pants had probably gotten him kidnapped. Austin had suffered through so many flashbacks today; maybe that was why they didn't stop now.

A FEW DAYS later, the cuffs were back on, the medical kit and the keys had been returned, and both men were out of the woods for this time. They could move around as long as they were careful, and there was no fever.

"You think this could ever be in fashion?" Austin joked dryly as he put on his sweats. Not only were they dirty, but there were several small tears after the torturer's knife. "My father would probably cry if he saw his pants destroyed like this."

That was obviously not true, but it was a running joke in their family; Austin's dad was extremely proud of his company. He ran a successful construction business which he'd built from the ground up, and this was a man who bought fancy cases to keep his business cards protected.

One time, Austin's mother had to put her foot down, because his dad wanted to buy pillowcases with the company logo on them. And for Christmases and birthdays, Griffin Huntley handed out pens, clothes, towels, coffee mugs, trucker caps, and notepads—all with the logo on them—as extra presents. The entire Huntley family was a walking ad for G.H. Construction.

A pang of sadness hit Austin squarely in the chest at the thought of his parents. He missed them terribly and couldn't imagine how upset his mother was. Maggie was the kind of woman who'd smack you upside the head with one hand and serve you apple pie with the other.

"Why would your pop care?" Cam looked puzzled. "Does he do your shopping or somethin'?"

Austin snorted. "That'd be a sight. But no." He pointed to the logo along his right leg. "My dad's business."

Cam studied Austin for a beat, then nodded pensively. "Yeah, that makes sense. You don't really strike me as a construction worker."

Austin didn't know whether to be offended or flattered. "What's that supposed to mean?" Okay, so it came out a bit defensive.

"At ease, soldier," Cam drawled with a lazy smirk. "I'm just saying you're not as, uh, mellow? I don't fucking know. You just come off a little more stiff than some handyman." He nodded as he thought of something. "I could see you in a suit."

Austin decided he was definitely offended. The image of a man in a suit wasn't usually followed by the words fun, adventurous, or carefree. Or mellow. A suit came with labels of dull, starched, and uptight.

Then again, wasn't Austin all those things? Maybe not uptight, but he did find his life rather calm and on-schedule. But at the same time, he couldn't recall missing any action. He led a safe life. Contentment and comfort.

Cam would probably add "boring as fuck."

"I'm an accountant," *Austin muttered and sat down on his cot.*

"Oh, yeah," *Cam chuckled.* "Now, that *fits." He grinned and scratched his brow. "I bet you wear suits for that."*

Austin gave him a wry look. "Well, it wouldn't look good if the office managing partner showed up in a Hawaiian shirt."

"Partner, huh?" *Cam nodded.* "Fancy."

Austin shrugged modestly. Numbers had always come easily for him. He liked the occasional challenge, and since tax laws always changed, he had to stay on top of things. His years in college weren't exactly enough. There was always something new to study.

His passion for his job had fizzled and died years ago, but he found comfort in structure and order.

"It's really not," *Austin replied eventually.* "The company's based in LA, so it's just a field office we have in Bakersfield." *And there was only one client: Kern County.* "Anyway…" *He wanted to change the topic now.* "What about you? Mechanic?" *He jerked his chin at Cam's coveralls.*

In retrospect, the men could say this was where their friendship began. After months of being locked up together, they started to get to know each other. To pass time, they shared memories and told one another about family members and hobbies.

Austin particularly enjoyed hearing the stories behind Cam's tattoos, mainly the ones that represented his disorder. There was a snowflake because it was said that people who had autism and Asperger's were like snowflakes— unique, one of a kind. The two words "wired differently" described Cam. It was also a part of a quote about Asperger's. Cam said, "We're not stupid. We're just wired differently." There were a few dark puzzle pieces that represented autism awareness. There were lyrics, sheet music, and instruments… everything came with an anecdote, a memory, or a reason.

AUSTIN SHIFTED BETWEEN nightmares, more pleasant memories, and consciousness. Too upset to find rest, too exhausted to rouse fully, too overwhelmed to make sense of everything that rolled like a movie behind his closed lids.

In one dream, his fingers brushed over Cam's tattoos. In another, he was on the floor in that cell, and he was fucking Cam brutally, which had certainly never happened in reality. Then the dreams morphed into group sessions with Gale where they all tried to make sense of their kidnapper's motives. Even with a profiler from the FBI on the case, they still only had an educated guess as to why that madman had kidnapped them.

Before long, the dream became a nightmare once more. The torture always came back.

Torture and death.

CHRIS HAD BEEN silent in his cell for two days before the other guys found out he had killed himself the same way James had—by slitting his wrists and swallowing the blades.

One cell was now empty. Chris and Pete both gone. Lance had been alone in his cell after James's death.

Their captor whistled a happy tune as he dragged Chris's body out of the basement, and before he disappeared, he told the others he had a performance review meeting planned with "Scott" later.

Scott's real name was Sean, and he shared a cell with Tim right next to Cam and Austin.

They all knew the outcome.

Not a thing to be done about that.

To be sure, though, Austin did search their cell for the umpteenth time, and this time Cam actually helped. Was there really no way out? Was it possible for a single man to keep ten others hostage? Now seven...

"Do you think we're still in Bakersfield?" Cam asked quietly, checking the bolts by the toilet. He tried to wiggle the toilet, but the solid chrome didn't budge a millimeter.

"No idea, but I have a better question for you." Austin was on his back on the floor, looking under his cot. "Do you think people are still searching for us?"

"Dude, they fucking better be."

NAMES AND BLURRY faces danced in the edges of Austin's vision; the nightmares held him hostage much like the madman had. Cam, Evan, Austin, Sam, Chase, Remy, Sean, Scott... there were too many names, and only half of them belonged to the guys in captivity.

The other names... well, they'd gotten their answers about that.

But why didn't the insane fucker torture the real Sam? Why didn't he beat the real Evan senseless instead of Cam? Why pretend with ten innocent men?

HOURS LATER, A nearly unconscious Sean was returned to his cell.

What hit Austin the hardest was how Sean cried out for his children while Tim tended to his wounds.

Sitting down on the floor, Austin pulled up his knees and dropped his forehead to them. He wanted Sean to stop—to shut up and suffer silently. Because all he did now was make Austin want to cry for his own daughter.

While Austin missed his wife, too, it was different when it came to his child. It wasn't until Riley was born that Austin understood his mother's words about the bond between a child and a parent being unbreakable. Friends could leave, wives and husbands could divorce, passion could fade, but the love you felt for your child was forever.

Maggie rarely spoke about the youngest son she lost to leukemia when Austin was ten years old, but that didn't mean he was forgotten. She religiously visited Riley's grave, the photos were never coming off the walls, and she loved him as if he were still alive.

The day Austin's daughter was born and he announced he was naming her after his younger brother, Maggie had been proud, not sad.

"You can't lose hope, man," Cam said, sitting down next to him. "Keep hoping you'll see her soon."

Austin was thankful Cam didn't make any promises. He wasn't sure he was strong enough to listen to vows neither man could keep.

"I think I've missed her birthday," he mumbled, discreetly tilting his

head to wipe away tears on his shoulder.

"When is it?"

"May fifth."

There was a smile in Cam's voice when he spoke next. "A Mexican celebration kid, huh?" He cautiously placed his arm around Austin's shoulders.

"Yeah." Austin sniffled and managed to pull off a small smile, but he kept his eyes downcast. "She loves Mexican food, too. And we wouldn't hear the end of it if her birthday didn't come with a piñata."

In fact, it was only recently Riley found out Cinco de Mayo *wasn't all about her. That had been a glum day, but it had brightened when Austin took her out for chips and salsa and queso. The girl was crazy about her queso.*

All this hurt to think about, especially when it felt like he had one foot in the grave already.

In a moment of defeat and despair, Austin leaned back and sought out Cam's shoulder to rest his head on. All curled up, he felt small and weak.

The thought didn't cross his mind, but it was Cam's bad shoulder. However, Cam didn't say a word; instead he silently encouraged Austin to lean on him, take comfort from him *for once, and rested his cheek on the top of Austin's head.*

AUSTIN HAD OF course missed Riley's tenth birthday. He didn't know what he'd been doing the day Riley turned ten, because time didn't give the men anything in that basement. Time only took from them. It had taken hope, strength, dignity, and humanity.

It wasn't until toward the end that things changed, and that was where clothes and professions played the biggest part. It was what finally gave the men something to mull over. Reasons, motives… but still more questions.

Cam's nickname for Austin had been coined one day…

"BREAKFAST!" MR. INSANE BELLOWED.

"I'd like to see the menu," Cam muttered as he got up from his cot to wait for the hatch to open. "I swear to Christ, I ain't never having chicken soup again if I ever get outta this place."

He flexed his bicep and shoulder, and Austin watched him wincing at the lingering pain, but at least it was getting better.

"I think I've forgotten what pizza tastes like." Austin sighed and emptied the bucket of water into the toilet.

They'd already washed their clothes as well as they could, and Cam's coveralls and Austin's torn sweats were currently drying on the floor. These days, though, they did it without soap. It had been a while since that one bar they'd been given was gone, and they hadn't been supplied with more.

The toothpaste was also gone, but they still had their toothbrushes.

"Even my shit smells like chicken nowadays," Cam said.

Austin didn't know whether to scoff or laugh. "No, it doesn't." He limped over to Cam, his right thigh still killing him, and gave him a sideways look. "Trust me. It does not smell like chicken."

Cam chuckled. "Fuck you."

Austin smirked and turned to the door as Psycho slid open the hatch.

"Evan. Sam." The crazy man smiled like a creep. "You seem to be

recovering nicely." Austin held up the empty bucket, and Mr. Crazy started filling it with the garden hose. "That's good—means I can plan our next meetings soon."

Cam gritted his teeth and glared.

"I think one meeting was enough," Austin said flatly, setting down the filled bucket on the floor.

"Oh, but it never is with uneducated simpletons." The man laughed and extended two bowls of steaming chicken broth. "I am your boss, fellas. I know what's best for you. After all, I didn't get this position by being stupid."

Cam took the bowls and huffed quietly. "No, just criminally insane."

"Yeah, and I thought having an MBA from Duke would save me from being called an uneducated simpleton," Austin drawled, only for Cam to hear.

Evidently, he hadn't been quiet enough.

"A what from where?" their kidnapper growled. His beady eyes turned murderous, and they were fixed on Austin.

Cam stiffened.

Austin frowned, but before he could respond, the hatch closed and they were left in a wake of furious screaming about ruined plans and how only accomplished people deserved to live.

"What the hell just happened?" He turned to Cam with a confused expression.

"You're asking me, Mr. MBA?" Cam snorted and shook his head. "Sometimes I find it hard to understand sane people."

AUSTIN WHIMPERED IN his sleep. Tears rolled down, unbeknownst to him. His body was tense with frustration.

Between the moments where the nightmares took over, family members asked him questions he couldn't answer. If given the choice, would he go back in time and put on a suit, hence saving himself from being kidnapped? It was his wife who asked. His mother asked if this could ever be worth it. His daughter just cried and cried and cried. Austin tried to reach out to her, but the image of Riley vanished with her heart-wrenching sobs.

TWO WHOLE DAYS went by without a glimpse of the madman. That meant two days without food and water. Two days that had been spent pacing, stewing in filth and boredom, and throwing out theories about their kidnapper's motives.

Austin was frustrated, feeling like there was more info to be had if they just hit the right angle.

They were all mostly on the same page, and they had been from the beginning. But with time, more things had surfaced. From the get-go, everyone had been assigned a character, and it hadn't taken long for the men to understand that each character represented someone from the torturer's real life. There was a father, two brothers, an old boss, a high school nemesis, a friend who had apparently betrayed him, a guy who was seemingly married to an old crush of the kidnapper, an uncle, and two cousins.

It all looked like vengeance, but it was executed on the wrong people. Instead of taking his anger out on those he'd grown up with or whatever, the insane man had kidnapped ten innocent strangers.

During these past two days, to pass time, a few of the remaining men had delved deeper into their theories. They went at it from different perspectives, first coming up with things that might tie them together—both to each other and to the kidnapper's family. It couldn't be age, though. Because Pete, who'd been shot in the head and had been assigned the character of the kidnapper's father, had to have been more ten years younger than the crazy man himself.

They guessed he was around fifty years old, and Pete had been thirty-six. In fact, all of the men were most likely younger than Psycho, as Cam had named him months ago.

Chris, who had killed himself not long ago, had been the oldest at forty-four, still younger than the kidnapper.

"Where did you all grow up?" Chase asked, and so they continued trying to piece everything together. One had grown up in New York, most were from Bakersfield, a couple were from LA, and one guy was from Portland.

No connections there, unless it fit with the kidnapper's family and friends.

"Our fucking jobs," Cam blurted out with a frown. "Yeah, think about it." He snapped his fingers. "What kinds of jobs do we all hold?"

But before anyone could ponder further, the madman was back in the basement.

"Attention, little minions!" he shouted. "It seems we've got a problem on our hands, and like a good boss, I'm here so we can fix it."

Austin and Cam exchanged a wary look as they leaned forward on their cots and rested their elbows on their knees, listening intently.

"Who has college experience?" the madman asked impatiently.

There was a brief silence before one spoke up. "Why the fuck should we answer, you twisted—"

Mr. Whoever-the-hell cut the man off. "I shoot! How about that, you brainless lowlife?"

Another silence ensued, this one tense.

Then the men began to answer—one by one, hesitantly. Most of them had gone off to college at some point. A few to two-year programs at community colleges to get associate's degrees, another few held bachelor's degrees. When Cam quietly announced he had a bachelor's, too, Austin curiously asked in what.

He was more than a little surprised when he heard Cam's answer.

"Theology," he mumbled, appearing slightly embarrassed. Just a second later, he squared his shoulders, as if getting ready to defend himself.

But Austin wasn't about to go on the offensive. He was just surprised and intrigued. Besides, the madman was waiting for his response, so he sighed and said, "Did my undergrad at USC Marshall, then got my MBA at Duke." Back in his day, it wasn't named Marshall School of Business, but it was what people knew it as today. Which made him feel a little old.

The last one to answer was Tim. "I have one year left to get my master's in engineering."

That made the madman explode for some reason. "But you're a fucking mailman!" he roared. "You're wearing your uniform!"

Austin eyed Cam's work clothes and couldn't help but wonder if they were all wearing some kind of uniform. But then he remembered two of the guys didn't have jobs, so there couldn't be a connection there, either.

What the hell was the crazy guy's obsession with work and education, though?

"It's to pay for school, idiot," Tim grunted. "I decided to change careers when I already had a family. I needed a fuckin' income. Christ."

Outside the cells, the men could hear the sounds of furious pacing, some kicking around, and a few fists being slammed into walls.

Cam was rigid.

Austin was exhausted. They were being toyed with, and there was only so

157

much he could take before he broke. Or gave up. It had been months with no glimpse of freedom in sight.

"Looks like I have to rework a few things," their captor said flatly. "It will take too long to replace all of you, but…" It appeared he was talking to himself, and Austin didn't know what to make of his words. "Sam and Frank are done, that much is clear." He spoke of Austin's and Tim's characters, which terrified both men, not to mention Cam, judging by the look on his face. "Then… bachelor's degrees… fairly good, but most have failed later. Still… educated…" He let out a growl. "I'll have to start over. This cannot be half-assed."

Before he stormed off, he announced, "Thank you for your cooperation, but this is the end. I have one meeting left—with Sam and Frank—and then it's time to terminate the project." He paused. "By project, I mean you. All of you." Lastly, there was a smile in his voice. "How do you feel about fire?"

AUSTIN SHOT UP from the bed and gasped for air while tears streamed down his face.

He was sure he could smell the gasoline.

THIRTEEN

CAM WAS ALMOST home, having walked Bourbon and picked up two burritos, when he saw a man about to ring the doorbell. Because Austin was asleep inside, Cam sped up.

"Can I help you?" he asked irritably.

He vaguely recognized the man as a neighbor from farther down the street. He was around Cam's age, maybe a few years younger, not very tall, slim, his dark hair a lot shorter on the sides than at the top of his head, plenty of ink and piercings, and looked like a mix between a skateboarder and a punk rocker.

"Sorry," the guy said, sticking his hands down into the pockets of his baggy chinos. "I didn't mean to disturb. I tried to call you earlier."

Cam raised a brow. Maybe this had been the anonymous caller, and it made sense. His home phone number was unfortunately listed, but his cell phone number wasn't. Though, if

159

this dude had been calling, he could've gotten the number from the contact sheet that everyone on the block had.

"I live down the street," he went on uncomfortably. "I'm trying to get in touch with Chase Gallardo—"

"Not interested," Cam snapped abruptly. Fucking hell, when were people gonna let this go? Idiots were still trying to contact all the surviving men for interviews, and they despised the attention. These were regular men who just wanted to get on with their lives.

Cam couldn't say he was close to the other guys, Chase included, but he did see them once every other week for their group session with Gale.

"Please wait," the guy practically begged. "I need to talk to him—to apologize."

That made Cam turn his head. With one hand on the door handle, he stared at the younger guy, who appeared to be fighting tears. He hid behind a stony mask of anger, but Cam saw guilt and desperation there, too.

"I was contacted by the police a few weeks ago," the guy explained, stumbling over his words. "Several people in my family were. But it wasn't until yesterday that a few details about the investigation were made public." Cam had shut out everything about the case, 'cause he saw no reason to follow the damn investigation. It wasn't like there'd be a trial or anything. Now they were just trying to piece things together, and regardless of how plausible each theory was, they'd never get solid proof. "I found out who Chase Gallardo was supposed to be when you were kidnapped—" he released a shaky breath "—by my half-brother."

Cam clenched his jaw, willing himself to calm down. It was

probably the fury in his eyes that made the other guy take a step back. "Who are you, exactly?" he asked in an eerily calm voice.

"My name is Remy." He said it as if it was a crime to carry that name. "Remy Stahl."

Cam nodded jerkily. Chase had been given the name Remy in that basement. It was Psycho's little brother. "Half-brother?"

"Yes." The guy, Remy, tugged at the piercing in his lip, and now he kept his eyes downcast. "My—our... father had an affair with-with my mom." Perhaps that could explain the age gap, 'cause Remy couldn't be much older than thirty, and Psycho had to have been in his late forties or fifties; plus, he had an older brother, to boot. "Look, I didn't come here to start trouble or anything. I barely have any contact with my family, but I wanna apologize to Chase..." He trailed off, still looking guilty.

Cam guessed it was survivor's guilt of whatever-the-fuck he could call it.

"I don't have his number," Cam said. "Don't know where he lives, either. But..." He hesitated for a beat. "I'm gonna see him next week." They had a group session on Tuesday. He could mention this to Chase then.

Remy nodded and let out a breath. "I'll understand if he doesn't wanna see me. Is it all right if I drop off a letter for him?"

Cam didn't really see the harm in that. "I guess."

BOURBON WAS QUICK to run into the kitchen to drink, and Cam went for the fridge to get some drinks, too. They'd only been out for a couple hours, but because Cam hadn't really eaten—he didn't count the scrambled eggs that tasted like shit—he was fucking starving now.

After leaving Austin's burrito in the kitchen, he took his own and a soda and headed for the patio. But when he reached the living room, he stopped short at the sight of the empty bed. Again, he'd only been gone a couple hours, which meant Austin hadn't slept long. At all.

"Austin?" he called out. He didn't get a response, but when he walked down the hall toward the bathroom, he heard the shower running. "You okay in there?"

"Yeah." Austin's voice was nearly drowned out by the sound of water. *"I'll be out soon."*

Cam frowned, then told himself he was worrying for nothing, and went outside.

While he sat at the table, shielded by the umbrella, he ate in silence and mulled over the weird meeting with Remy Stahl. He didn't really know what to make of it, though, so he just shook it off. Maybe if he'd been closer to Chase, he'd have an opinion. All Cam really knew about Chase was that he was a thirty-six-year-old bartender; he was quiet and reserved.

"Shit." Cam rubbed at his chest, having eaten too fast. Again. More Pepto were definitely coming his way.

Pulling his T-shirt over his head, he dropped it in the chair next to him, then fished out his smokes. Around that time, Austin joined him, too, only wearing a towel around his hips. Cam told him there was food for him in the kitchen, so Austin disappeared for a minute, only to return with his burrito.

"Thank you," Austin said quietly, kissing the top of Cam's head. Then he sat down on the other side of table, and Cam saw that his eyes were bloodshot behind his glasses. "What? Do I have something on my face?"

Cam pursed his lips and shook his head minutely. "Couldn't sleep?"

It was Austin's turn to shake his head. "Nightmares." He unwrapped his burrito and seemed to be struggling to keep his breathing even.

"You can talk to me about it," Cam offered carefully.

"The last night," Austin whispered, looking down at his food. "I can't shake the smell of gasoline."

Cam swallowed hard and turned his gaze to the covered pool.

In many ways, the last night in captivity was the absolute worst.

CAM HAD PICTURED his final meal to be a bit more extravagant than the usual chicken soup, stale bread, and lukewarm milk. Not that it really mattered. He had no appetite what-so-fucking-ever.

The newly-added smell in the basement didn't help. A while ago, Psycho had poured gasoline on the floor. It was slowly seeping inside the cells, and the fumes were making everyone dizzy and nauseous.

"You should eat," Austin mumbled automatically.

Cam shook his head, seated on his cot, and stared down into his bowl. After yesterday's announcement from the goddamn psycho, the only thing he could stomach was water.

"Cam…"

"He's gonna set this fucking place on fire," Cam whispered, not lifting his eyes to face his friend. *"We're gonna burn alive."*

So far, Psycho had followed through on every goddamn promise. He wasn't afraid to use his gun, and he seemed to get his rocks off in torturing others. There was no reason to believe this was just a scare tactic. If anything, the heavy odor of the gasoline only proved he was planning to set it all on fire.

"I don't want to think about that." Austin's voice was thick. *"Besides—"* he tried and failed to brighten his tone *"—first, I have a meeting to look forward to."*

Cam set down the bowl of soup. There was no fucking way he'd eat it. He felt sick to his stomach, and his body ached after these months of captivity and torture. *"Do you think he'll take you and Tim at once? He only mentioned one 'meeting.' 'Cause if it is the both of you…"* He was grasping at straws, but what else was he gonna do? *"Maybe you can take him."*

Austin's mouth twisted into a small grimace. *"Didn't work when we tried, Cam."* He sighed. *"I'm not going to give up an opportunity if it presents itself, but I'm not counting on it. He's been too meticulous. He drugged us to get us here, cuffed us to slow us down… he gives out food with only enough nutrition to keep us alive, and he has that gun, which he's used more than once."* His eyes met Cam's as they both looked up. *"I honestly don't know how much physical strength I have left. I'm constantly tired, and…"* He trailed off and averted his eyes. *"I don't know. I don't think there's any hope left."*

Cam forced a smile. *"I'm not sure how to deal with this."* As had been stated countless times before, he loathed showing weakness. But Austin had proved to be someone Cam didn't have to hide for. Austin hadn't treated him any differently just because he knew of Cam's disorders. At least not much.

Maybe he'd been a bit more patient and attentive, but he didn't treat Cam like something fragile, and he still didn't take his bullshit.

"I only have one suggestion." Austin put his food aside. Then he stood up and motioned for Cam to stand, too. They closed the distance between them and Austin moved his cuffed hands over Cam's head, then cupped his neck and rested their foreheads together. "I think it's time for empty promises."

Cam let out a soft breath and nodded in return, reveling in the sense of comfort all while his heart ached at the obvious surrender. Was this it? Had they come so far past believing in rescue that they had to lie to one another in order to cope and keep breathing?

"We'll m-make it out alive," he rasped. "You'll see your wife and daughter again, and I'll be under the hood of some vintage car." He smiled sadly, not really meaning for Austin to see, and tilted his head. "It'll be okay." His nose and lips brushed against the inside of Austin's forearm.

The tension crackled, both men desperate for any kind of closeness. The moment left them confused, but neither moved away for a long while.

Releasing a shaky breath, Austin dropped his forehead to Cam's shoulder. Cam felt as Austin ghosted his lips over his skin. A slow but forceful shiver ran down his spine, pressing heat closer to the surface.

"I'll try—" Austin's voice was threadbare and almost inaudible. "If I see a chance, I'll fight with all I have left."

Those words both soothed and terrified Cam. "Gun or no gun?"

"Gun or no gun."

CAM SQUEEZED HIS eyes shut as the "empty" promises echoed through him.

They'd made it out alive, but at that point, they really hadn't believed in an escape.

"Hey." Austin grabbed Cam's hand on the table. "I didn't mean to push my shit onto you."

"Stop." Cam shook his head and threaded their fingers together. "It's cool. I'm okay. I was just thinking…" That Austin had gotten what he wished for. He was back with his wife and daughter.

It was making Cam antsy as fuck to not know exactly what was going on between them. He trusted Austin with his life, and he knew Austin meant what he'd said—he didn't take any of this lightly. But that didn't really offer any answers. Austin was always gonna prioritize Riley, and while Cam could understand that— hell, he wouldn't have it any other way—it made him question things. For instance, would Austin stay with Jade for Riley's sake?

Even if he didn't, what was Cam ready for? They'd just returned to freedom; their lives were changed forever. Who knew how long they'd be picking up the pieces to put their lives back together. Cam needed his routines; he needed his stability. Then, on the other hand, he needed Austin, too. He wanted them in the same fucking bed at night.

Merely a few hours ago, he'd let Austin fuck him. And it had been… fucking amazing—no other words for it. He rarely bottomed, but that didn't mean he preferred to top. Well, he did, but bottoming was more intimate, in his opinion. It wasn't for casual hookups, which meant he hadn't bottomed since college. It was the last time he'd had a steady partner, and it hadn't ended dramatically with broken hearts or anything, but Cam decided casual was better for him. Opening up to another person wasn't easy, and it took time for Cam to trust. But with Austin?

Cam would do anything for that man.

I'm probably in love with the bastard.

Austin was about to say something when Cam heard a phone ring from inside. It wasn't his own, so he concluded it was Austin's. "Your phone's ringing," he said, reeling on the inside from his realization about his feelings.

Could that be it? Had he fallen for Austin?

"Oh. It's probably Riley." Austin stood up and went inside.

Cam sighed heavily and lit up a smoke, then started tapping his thumb together with his fingers.

WHEN AUSTIN GRABBED his phone off the coffee table, he was surprised to see his home number as caller ID.

Jade and Riley weren't supposed to be back from visiting Jade's parents in Delano until tomorrow.

"Hello?" He answered the phone, then immediately held it away from his ear when all he was met by were Riley's sobs. "Riley, what's wrong?" Austin was already heading down the hall to get his clothes from last night. "Talk to me, baby girl."

"I don't wan-wanna move, Daddy!" she wailed.

"What?" He frowned in confusion and pulled on his jeans. "I don't understand. Can you explain for me?"

Riley kept crying. *"Mom said we're gonna move! I don't wanna move to Delano! I-I have all my friends here!"* Austin froze. A mere second later, the phone was ripped away from Riley, and Jade's voice rang out. *"It's not what you think, Austin. Riley overheard me and my mother talking, so we left early—Look, can you just come home? Where the hell are you, anyway?"* Now she sounded annoyed.

"I…" Austin didn't know what to say. He was flabbergasted. "Uh—I'm with Cam." He shook his head as if to clear it. Then his anger was back in full force. "What the *fuck* is Riley talking about?" He pulled on his shirt, awkwardly buttoning it one-handed.

"It's nothing that should be discussed over the phone—Go to your room, Riley!" she yelled in the background. *"Hurry, Aust—"*

"I'll be there in twenty," he snapped and ended the call.

His mind was a jumbled mess, as per usual, but now there was a bunch of new shit. Jesus Christ, when was it all going to end? This day was proving to be both incredibly difficult to struggle through and… well, with Cam's presence it was manageable.

"Cam, I have to—" He broke off when he saw Cam standing in the hallway with his wallet and car keys. Austin sighed and walked closer. "Thank you," he said quietly, accepting his personal belongings. "Jade and Riley came home early. I have to go."

"I gathered that." Cam offered a forced smile. "Trouble in paradise?"

Austin snorted and put on his shoes. "More like the final nail in the coffin."

He scrubbed a hand over his face, bone-weary and angry. This was one of those times he didn't want to be an adult. Closing the distance between them, Austin dropped his forehead to Cam's shoulder.

"Tell me to come back." He needed to hear it—to hear that *something* was real.

Tension he hadn't even noticed before disappeared from Cam's shoulders. "Come back whenever you can," he murmured. "And, um, it's been a taxing day for you. You should probably take your meds."

Austin grinned tiredly and lifted his head. "We'll see." Leaning in, he kissed Cam but ended it too soon. "I'll call you."

FOURTEEN

THE MINUTE AUSTIN stepped foot inside his house, there was shouting from Jade and sobbing from Riley.

Austin had prepared himself on the ride over, though. He knew what was about to happen, so he took control. Walking in to the kitchen, he was spotted by Riley first, who threw herself at him.

"Are we really gonna move to Delano, Dad?" she cried.

"No. I promise." He hugged her tight and kissed the top of her head. "Now, go to your room while I talk to Mom."

"But—"

"Go," he commanded softly, and Riley slumped her shoulders and went upstairs to her room. Austin faced Jade next, wondering why they hadn't separated yet. It was clearly long overdue. "How long have you been thinking about divorce?" he asked bluntly. Because he couldn't believe this was new. He'd only been home for less than a month. A marriage didn't fall apart that quickly—not after fifteen years.

Jade swallowed, a flicker of regret flashing across her features. "The past year... I'm really sorry, Austin—"

"Don't apologize." Austin didn't want to hear it. "I should've seen it coming. God knows I see it now." He sat down at the table; Jade cautiously joined him. "But what's this crap about Delano?"

"I've been offered a job there," she admitted. "I want to take it."

Austin nodded, just wanting to get this over with. It was becoming abundantly clear to him that in order to heal, he needed to be by himself. Not counting his daughter.

"Riley stays with me."

Jade's eyes widened. "What? No!" she cried out. "I'm her mother; she should be with me."

A small and sinister smile made its way to Austin's face. "Wrong way to phrase it, Jade. She should be with you if you *want* her to. Not because you're her mother." Anger burned in his eyes. "How will you even deal with all this? You're just going to pack up the house, move to Delano, get settled in a new place, adjust to your new job, enroll Riley at a new school, *and* deal with the fact that she doesn't want to be there?"

Jade glared at him. "Don't drag this out. I want an easy divorce, and you being bitter won't help."

Austin couldn't help but laugh. "*Bitter?* Oh, Jade." He chuckled and shook his head. "You have it all wrong. You're under the impression that I want us to stay together." Jade suddenly looked shocked. "Truth be told, I honestly don't give a *fuck* about you anymore." That was aimed to hurt, and it looked like it did. But his ex-wife-to-be fucking deserved it. The way she'd treated him since he came back home… "You manipulative little…" He trailed off, angrier than ever before.

"Austin," Jade choked out. "What are you doing? How can you say that to me—"

"Asks the woman who told me to get over a five-month long kidnapping without so much as a pat on the back." Austin raised a brow. "You've used that as an excuse to get out, haven't you?" Jade didn't respond. But Austin didn't need her to. She'd never been a good liar; he could see the truth written on her face. "God, you're fucking selfish." He didn't want to think that about the woman he'd spent fifteen years being married to, but there it was. A few years of taking each other for granted and just going through the motions… Jade was right.

He was bitter. So was she.

"And my mom wonders why I resent you," Jade chuckled humorlessly through tears.

Austin stared at her long and hard, finding it difficult to stick with one emotion. Anger was the only one that persisted. Then there were fleeting moments of pity, sorrow, compassion, understanding, regret, and disappointment.

"If it's any consolation, I know I haven't been the best husband." He wanted to add that he'd at least stood by her side all these years, and up until he felt more drawn to Cam than Jade, it would've been true. But he didn't want to lie to Jade, though the reason was Cam. If Austin claimed he'd been nothing but faithful, it would be like denying what he'd started with Cam. He couldn't do that. He *wouldn't* do that.

"I'm sorry I pushed you to leave the past in the past," she muttered, not sounding particularly sincere. "I did use it against you—thought you'd leave before I could."

Manipulative was right.

That was where the majority of Austin's bitterness stemmed from. He felt betrayed. He'd gone through hell, and Jade had used it as an excuse to get the fucking ball rolling.

"Riley stays with me," he repeated. Now he was eager to get this over with. Even if a divorce took at least six months to be finalized in the state of California, they could separate immediately. "We'll divide all the assets, and I won't demand child support." He made more money than Jade, so the idea was ridiculous. "She can stay with you every other weekend, and whenever she wants to see you, I'll make it happen."

"It's not right," Jade gritted out. "If anything, we should ask her." She almost looked smug.

It proved that Jade didn't know her own daughter as well as she liked to think.

Riley was Daddy's girl. Through and through.

THAT NIGHT, AUSTIN sat in the chair by the window in Riley's room after she'd cried herself to sleep. Despite the obvious resentment and hostility between Austin and Jade, they'd managed to cool off before they sat down like responsible adults and told

Riley that Mom and Dad were getting divorced.

Riley had reacted like any other ten-year-old girl would; she'd been inconsolable. Mom and Dad were supposed to stay together—end of story. But, thankfully—depending on how you looked at it—she was old enough to know that some marriages didn't work out. It was a harsh reality, but she wouldn't be the first in her class to have divorced parents.

Spending time with her classmates had shown her both sides of the coin. There were parents who didn't get along after a split; their homes weren't as nice to be in—more fighting going on. There were parents who got along great; their kids grinned and said what it was like to have two birthdays, two rooms, and two Christmases. Then there were those friends of Riley's who had to deal with their parents remarrying…

Riley hadn't liked the idea of her parents finding new spouses.

Austin had been quick to divert, and he and Jade had then spent a long time explaining things as well as they could to a ten-year-old. It wasn't her fault. Sometimes adults drifted apart. No, Mom and Dad didn't hate each other. She could choose where she wanted to live. Mom and Dad would never hold any decision against her.

To Jade's credit, she'd hidden her disappointment very well when Riley said she didn't want to leave Bakersfield. While Austin had given them some privacy and went to call his parents, Jade and Riley had made loose plans about fun stuff they could do whenever Riley came to Delano.

Now Riley was asleep, and Austin could see the blotchiness around her eyes and the tears that had soaked her pillow.

This was only the beginning of a new era, and Austin didn't really know what to feel. For once, there was no anger, though. He was numb, but little sparks of relief flared up inside him every now and then. He was breaking free, something he'd done before. But in a very different setting.

"GUN" HAD BECOME plural when the madman returned to get Austin and Tim, but just because he held two guns didn't have to mean more of an upper hand. Because his focus was divided, and Austin prayed there would be at least one window of opportunity.

Austin and Tim didn't need to speak; a single look was enough for both to understand that this was more than likely their last chance. If they didn't put up a fight now, they might as well drop dead right here, right now. In fact, they were so consumed by this thought that they barely acknowledged that this was the first time they had seen each other. Austin just registered tall and wiry and dark. Whereas Austin would probably gain leverage in body impact, Tim had speed on his side.

"Let's go." The torturer walked backward up the narrow steps, aiming both guns at Austin and Tim, both of whom were cuffed behind their backs. "I hope you said goodbye to your buddies, because you won't see them again."

Austin didn't allow the panic to pull him under. He gritted his teeth and climbed the stairs at the same slow pace their kidnapper moved. Austin knew he wouldn't be able to fight worth a damn if he first had to suffer through another round of torture.

That left a couple opportunities: one when the password had to be punched in to open the door to the torture room, and one if the crazy man had plans to restrain them in said room. He wouldn't be able to do that while keeping an eye on both Austin and Tim.

Tim seemed to be thinking the same thing, because he subtly nudged his shoulder to Austin's when they approached the top of the landing.

Meanwhile, Mr. Insane was focusing so intently that sweat began to trickle down his neck, appearing under the mask. "No funny business," he said, pushing the heavy door open.

Austin and Tim bided their time, not wanting this fight to happen mere inches away from a fall down the stairs. Their eyes were fixed on the man who had taken them from their families months prior.

This was it. They had to take this chance, or create it.

Perhaps their kidnapper was getting cocky, because this was a grave mistake. He clearly wasn't aware of just how unafraid these guys had become of the prospect of getting shot. Tim and Austin had nothing to lose. Really, the crazy man should've brought them upstairs one by one.

When they reached the little vestibule with three other doors, Austin and Tim took a collective breath as they watched their target slowly reach out to the keypad, though he still kept his eyes on Austin and Tim.

But there was that one flicker of a second where the kidnapper had to make sure he'd punched in the correct code.

Gun or no gun, Austin and Tim charged.

Austin was crazed with fury and desperation as he rammed into the madman. He heard the shot that rang out, but he barely registered the bullet piercing his flesh, lodging deeply in his bicep. He barely felt the shocking pain that exploded and spread throughout his body, either.

The taste of possible freedom overrode any fear.

With his shoulder pressing forcefully into their kidnapper's collarbone, Austin slammed his forehead against the man's nose, causing him to stumble back. The trigger was pulled again, and Tim shouted a curse. But Tim wasn't deterred, either. While Austin pinned the psycho and tried to harm him however possible, Tim struggled to get the guns, which wasn't easy without use of his hands.

A third shot echoed painfully loud in the small space just as Austin managed to put all his body weight into a shove that broke the madman's arm against a doorframe. It bent in an odd way, a hoarse scream filling the air, and one gun dropped to the ground.

Before they could free their hands, Tim just kicked the gun aside and went to the other side to get the second gun.

"Justice will prevail!" the kidnapper screamed.

"Count on it," Austin growled, struggling to keep the man pinned to the wall. "You sick bastard." Fatigue and pain were quickly taking over, but he refused to surrender now. Through the closed door that led to the basement, they could hear the shouts of their fellow captives. "Jesus Christ." The man managed to knee Austin in the gut, though Tim defended him by ramming his shoulder into the kidnapper's throat. It was a good thing he was so freaking tall.

"Sam and Frank deserve to die." Mr. Crazy's voice was a choked breath.

"We're not them!" Tim shouted and finally managed to get control of the second gun. It was dropped to the floor, and without wasting time, he and Austin pulled their prey down to the ground. "Sit on him."

Austin did better than that. His ass hit the ground and he planted his elbow into the madman's upper back. Austin's arms burned, his hands aching to be free, but this had to do for now. The kidnapper was facing the floor, several feet away from his guns, and he had a sharp elbow keeping him in place.

So, while Austin made sure their captor couldn't move, Tim moved around in search of the keys.

"This isn't over," the madman wheezed out.

"That's for damn certain," Austin grunted. "You're still breathing."

"Found them!" Tim fished something out of their kidnapper's back pocket, which turned out to be the keys for the handcuffs. "I fucking found them!"

FIFTEEN

CAM RUBBED HIS wrists, now free from the bandages, as he waited for Gale to start the group session. Due to his appointment at the hospital, he was early, but a few of the other guys were already here, too. Chase was one of them, and Cam had given him Remy's letter just to have it over with. He'd explained briefly that Remy had contacted him, wanting to get in touch with Chase, and that was that. Now, Chase was sitting on the other side of the waiting room outside Gale's office, staring quietly at the unopened envelope.

"Huntley's not coming?" Victor asked, probably 'cause Cam and Austin usually showed up together.

Cam shook his head no and drummed his fingers on his thigh. He didn't feel like talking, so he didn't. But that didn't mean he wasn't thinking about Austin's reason for not being here. 'Cause he sure as fuck was.

Austin hadn't shown up again on Saturday, nor on Sunday, nor on Monday. But they'd kept in touch through texts and calls, and Cam knew all about the separation and the divorce.

He couldn't deny it; he was relieved for selfish reasons. Whenever Austin called him, ranting, bitching, yelling... just unloading, Cam was merely satisfied it was to him. Apparently, it was pretty frosty between Austin and Jade, though they maintained a united front for Riley's sake, and now they were rushing to move on from each other.

Jade was gonna move in with her parents in Delano for a while 'til she found her own place. First, she was gonna get settled in at her new job, which she started in three weeks, according to Austin. And today, she was having a girls' day with Riley. Austin had told him that they were gonna make copies of all their home movies, make scrapbooks of photos that didn't have albums, and... some other shit. Meanwhile—the reason Austin had to cancel on today's group session—he was gonna look at an apartment not far from where Cam lived.

One reason for the rush, other than the fact that Austin and Jade wanted to get this over with, was that Riley started her new school year soon, and Austin wanted to be settled before then. So, he wasn't picky—as long as Riley could have her own room. It was supposedly temporary, this apartment business, but Cam hadn't asked any further questions. He was just stoked Austin was looking at apartments near Cam's house.

Thinking ahead, he realized that meant a new school district for Riley, so that could also be a reason to hurry. Changing schools was never fun, but it would suck even more if it happened once the semester had already started.

As far as Cam knew, Riley's only demands were to stay in Bakersfield with her dad and that she would be relatively close to her old friends.

Just as Sean showed up and nodded in hello, Cam's phone vibrated with an incoming text from Austin.

Can I spend the night at your house? Tomorrow, too. Jade's turning the house into a showcase home for the Realtor's photographer, and my parents are picking up Riley in a few hours.

They really weren't wasting time, Cam mused as he typed out a response.

It'll cost ya.

The reply was almost instant.

The Realtor or spending the night with you? I think I can manage.

Cam grinned to himself and pocketed the phone. He hoped he'd see Austin soon, like right after this session. They both had a lot to do today, but because Austin had to cancel now, he'd made an appointment with Gale for right after. Seeing each other in passing wouldn't hurt.

Later today, Cam was driving over to the garage his brother owned. Having never been a big spender, he still had plenty of savings, but he missed getting his hands dirty. He missed the smell, and he missed the tinkering. It had always taken care of his fidgeting in the past. To see a car roll in, then locate the issue and fix it—yeah, he fucking yearned to go back. Especially with old cars, the vintage beauties. Not that they didn't cater to others; it was a big garage, and Landon had a crew who knew a lot.

Whether it was big trucks with air-brake system failure after a cross-country drive, motorcycles in need of brake pad replacement, vintage cars where the ignition sometimes gave you trouble since yesterday's technology wasn't as advanced, or tow service, Landon's guys could handle it. And Cam had his own nook in the large service bay where he took on problems that made the others throw in the towel.

For someone who lost his patience so quickly, he had it in abundance when it came to cars. He *understood* cars. There was logic in engines. It was black and white.

Once upon a time, Cam had studied theology for five years to understand religion, and he still hadn't gotten his fucking answers. His parents were religious to the point where they went to church on holidays, and Jules had grown up in a strict Catholic family, though no one could really tell even if they knew her. But Cam couldn't see the big deal. He relied on science, straight answers, and logic. He had tried, though. No one could say he hadn't.

And if religion was bad, what could he say about psychology? Christ, he really hated coming here, though it was necessary. He might not understand how Gale helped, but she did nonetheless. After some sessions, he felt raw and turned inside out, but it kept him sane. The way past pain was through it. Bottling it up would destroy him.

"Did youse read the interview in yesterday's paper?" Lance asked. He'd been the last to arrive, and Cam knew this was his last session. He'd decided to move back to New York, back to Staten Island, and who could blame him? Lance had moved here for a job in construction two years ago; that probably wasn't enough to outweigh the bad memories he now lived with.

After all that time in a basement that smelled of mildew, Lance had even become asthmatic.

Some of the guys murmured yes; they'd read the interview, but Cam tuned it out. He knew all too fucking well that Psycho's older brother and mother were throwing around kind words like propaganda. He didn't need to read the details.

"The bitch said he was a straight-A student and a perfect son," Victor said, scoffing. "Perfect, my ass."

It was like this before every group session. The guys would gossip and curse about the interviews, and Cam and Austin would sit there in silence, trying to ignore it all. Actually, Chase was quiet, too. Cam's own theory about Chase's silence was that he felt guilty—for a stupid goddamn reason—'cause he hadn't seen the inside of that torture room. He wasn't the only one who hadn't. Cam figured they should just see it as a small blessing, but, re-fucking-gardless, they'd been through hell, too.

Cam shook his head and looked down at the scars on his wrists. Blessing. *There's some divine shit right there.* Fucking religion.

"Yo, Cam." Lance jerked his chin. "Where's Austin?"

"Elsewhere," Cam said flatly.

He didn't particularly like these guys. Then again, he didn't like many.

Thankfully, Gale opened the door to her office then, saving him from *chit-chat*. There were few things worse than meaningless conversation.

"Come on in, guys." She smiled, flashing white teeth with lipstick traces.

As always, Cam sat down in the loveseat in the corner—where

Austin usually sat with him—and he avoided getting close to anyone else. The office wasn't very big, so it was a tight fit when seven, now six, other dudes crammed themselves in. Gale sat down in front of her desk, Tim and Sean occupied a small couch, Lance and Victor in two chairs, and Chase sat down on the floor by the door, even though there were a couple more chairs available.

To Cam's knowledge, only Tim and Sean, who'd been cellmates, had formed a bond much like Cam and Austin had—although he doubted theirs was more than friendship. Chase, for instance, had shared his cage with Victor, but there was no attachment of any kind.

"Last time, we talked about the two days at the end where you were left without food and water," Gale said, clasping her hands over her notepad. "Today I thought we could talk about your last night." Her gaze traveled to Cam, and she smiled gently. "Oh, that's right. Austin isn't here." She then looked to Tim. "Why don't you start? You and Austin managed to gain the upper hand."

Cam fiddled with his phone as Tim reluctantly recalled the events that ultimately led to their escape. Cam wasn't really doing anything with that fucking phone, but he needed to keep his fingers occupied. He was forced to listen, and each man had different recollections of that night. Cam himself remembered the dread as he'd waited and hoped to see Austin alive.

CAM PACED BY the door to the cell, tears streaming down his cheeks, not

that he really noticed. He was too busy trying to breathe.

He'd heard three shots ring out, and there had been commotion for several minutes after.

Did he even dare hope Austin was still alive?

"He better be." He wiped his damp cheek against his shoulder, cursing the cuffs behind his back. "He fucking better be."

A couple things didn't add up. Firstly, Cam hadn't heard a single noise from the times others had been tortured, yet he could clearly hear something now. Secondly, the shots confused him since they were followed by thumps, shouts, and what appeared to be bumping into walls.

Cam hated how fucking desperate he was—that he was hanging on to a few odds and ends which could mean a struggle with a new outcome. 'Cause it could, couldn't it? The fact that he could hear some kind of fight had to mean they were closer, that they weren't in the torture room, right? And Cam couldn't imagine Psycho "planning" the torture just outside the door on the first floor. Or wherever they were.

"Tim and Austin are fighting him—that has to be it," Sean said, though he didn't sound very confident. "We can't die down here. They gotta fight him."

"Shut the fuck up!" Cam kicked the door. "Like it's their fucking responsibility? That's funny, dude—'cause I haven't seen you even try to put up a fight."

"Whoa, I didn't mean—"

"Whatever," Cam spat out. "Just keep your mouth shut." His head was pounding; the guys practically taking bets on what was going on only made it worse. Fuck. He needed to see Austin now.

And maybe, just maybe, after going through hell for however long, someone was finally granting wishes. 'Cause a minute or so later, the door leading to the basement was shoved open and Cam heard the sounds of two people walking down. No one was thrown down, and it wasn't just one person. Two. Two people. Cam fucking prayed it was Austin. And Tim.

He held his breath when whomever was on the outside fiddled with the lock on the door to the cell. Which Psycho only did after checking the hatch first.

Time froze for Cam as Austin appeared in the open doorway, sweaty, grimy, blood sliding down his bicep, and only wearing those torn sweatpants of his. Both men looked like death warmed over, and shock was written across their filthy features.

"Austin," Cam finally choked out.

Austin didn't reply, but he did shuffle closer, his posture revealing he was in serious pain. When he reached Cam, he slid his arms around Cam's waist and dropped his forehead to his shoulder. Cam let out a shuddering breath, remaining quiet and barely breathing as Austin freed him of his cuffs.

"We did it."

"Christ." Cam threw his arms around Austin's neck, but he backed away immediately when Austin winced. "Your arm." He'd been shot. "Fuck, your arm, Austin."

"I'll survive," he replied with a small smile and touched their foreheads together.

More tears streamed down Cam's face, and he grinned through them.

Austin smiled back and winced as he brought up his hands to brush his thumbs under Cam's eyes.

Outside the cell, a few other men appeared, Tim having released them all.

"You really did it." Cam could barely believe it, much less let it settle inside him. "Where's…?"

Austin jerked his chin in the direction of the stairs. "We cuffed him upstairs—took his keys and guns, too." He blew out a breath. "We're going to lock him into one of these cells—"

"Why don't we just kill him?" Cam asked bluntly.

"Believe me—the thought crossed my mind. But we need the passwords to get out." Austin sighed and inspected his gunshot wound. "I think I'm in shock, because I can barely feel this. But I need to patch it up so I don't lose more blood." He smiled wryly at Cam. "Tim was shot in the foot—pissed him off like you wouldn't believe."

Cam ignored that and said, "We gotta find you a medical kit. And you mentioned guns; we could always fire off a couple rounds at the door. Maybe aim at the hinges or something."

He walked over to the water bucket, gently placing the soaked washcloth around the wrist that hurt the most from the cuffs. The fabric and the water were far from clean; he probably risked infection, but so did touching everything else down here, and he fucking needed the pain relief the chill of the water offered.

"If we get out without the douchebag's help, I wanna kill him."

"I think there's a line." Austin's mouth quirked up a little. "Come on—let's go talk to the others."

Because all the men were in a state of shock, they got a surprising amount done without emotions bringing them to their knees.

CAM GULPED AND gritted his teeth together. It was in complete silence, as Lance began to talk, that Cam tried to regain his breathing. Only Chase noticed; he side-eyed Cam a little, but he said nothing.

God-fucking-dammit. Cam despised this. But, he had to admit, it was getting better. The more he remembered, the more he got used to the onslaught of emotions. It didn't catch him off guard as easily as it had mere weeks ago.

"And as I understand it—Cam, you had a theory about why the ten of you were chosen," Gale continued patiently. "You talked about that while Victor, Sean, and Lance tried to get the door open."

Cam shrugged and let out a heavy breath. What Gale said wasn't exactly correct. They had all been on the same page about Psycho's motives. Cam had only connected the last dots, sort of. What had once been a guess became a solid theory with Cam's thoughts.

"I just said that shit about our clothes," Cam muttered. "It seemed plausible or whatever."

Austin tilted his head back, looking like he was dizzy, as Cam cleaned the bullet wound in his bicep. Like Cam had suggested, a couple of the guys had used the guns on the armored doors and managed to get one open. The bullets were all gone, but the door they did shoot open had turned out to be a supply closet. Medical kits, utensils, toilet paper, razors, toothbrushes, toothpaste... a lot of shit was found in there. But most importantly, they'd found a tool box and a crowbar, all of which Victor, Sean, and Lance were using to try to open the door that hopefully led to freedom. With the guns, they'd managed to do some damage, and now all they needed was that final shove.

In the meantime, Tim and Chase were guarding the crazy motherfucker who was now cuffed inside Chris and Pete's old cell. The reason they picked that cell was 'cause there was a pipe in one of the corners—a perfect spot to cuff Psycho to.

That left Cam and Austin seated on the stairs in the basement with a medical kit.

It felt so fucking odd to move around freely, even if they were still somewhat locked in. It was pretty dark, and the fumes from the spilled gasoline made things even worse. Still, it was a small slice of freedom.

"You shouldn't be alive!" Psycho cried out. "It's wrong! It's wrong!"

"Shut him up!" Cam growled, turning his head toward the cell. His hands on Austin's arm had stilled, but he didn't move them away. "I don't care; just, just—bash his fucking head in!"

"My pleasure," they heard Chase mutter. Soon, he was pounding on the kidnapper.

Cam sighed and returned to applying antiseptic cream to Austin's arm. "I was thinking," he said quietly. "What can you tell by looking at the other guys?"

Austin probably figured Cam was doing this to distract him from the pain. "Nothing. Other than they're just as beat-up and filthy as us."

Cam hummed. "Their clothes. They're all in work clothes—except for Sean, who's unemployed. Pete didn't have a job, either, but..." Pete wasn't alive, so that didn't really matter.

"I'm not in work clothes," Austin reminded him, then hissed when Cam placed a sterile pad on his wound. "Damn."

"Sorry. But yeah, you kinda are." Cam gave Austin's shredded sweatpants a pointed look. "Psycho picked you up when you were wearing pants with a logo from a construction company."

"All right." Austin conceded. "So? Where're you going with this?"

Instead of answering right away, Cam peered up the stairs. "Sean!" The incessant noise of three men trying to force open a heavy, steel door silenced for a beat. "What were you doing when that motherfucker took you?"

The silence went on for another moment before an obviously tired Sean replied. "I was coming out of a diner. Why?"

Cam's brow furrowed in concentration. Then he asked the next question. "What did you do before that? What did you do that day?"

"What?" Sean sounded confused. "What's with the Twenty Questions?"

"Just answer," Cam said quickly, impatiently.

He sensed Austin's smile and was sure it was 'cause Austin knew him by now—his temper, his impatience. For a second, Austin leaned closer to him, but then he frowned and leaned back again, quickly followed by a shake of his head.

"Before getting lunch," Sean continued, appearing to think back on the day he was kidnapped, "I'd picked up my son's tux—Valentine's Dance and all. And, uh… I was looking for work; I had a couple interviews lined up. Talked to the people down at the unemployment office—"

"That could be it." Cam snapped his fingers and nodded. Then he resumed patching up Austin's arm and lowered his voice. Sean was out of the conversation already. "So, imagine Psycho trying to find his next victim. He follows Sean, who looks like an average Joe, and hits the goddamn jackpot when Sean later unknowingly tells the world he doesn't have a job when he walks into that unemployment office." He paused to pay attention as he tore off a bit of medical tape and fastened it across Austin's skin. "When he's done, he's got a couple unemployed dudes, a couple construction workers, a mechanic, a mailman, a plumber… it goes on like that. No suits." He eyed Austin. "No Ivy League or other fancy colleges. No fucking success."

Austin arched a brow. "There's a lot of money in construction." And he went on about how he knew that for several reasons. Bakersfield was attractive mainly for the oil and agriculture industries, but also 'cause of its low sales tax, which led to many companies moving here—or there?—depending on where they were right now. Land was cheap, and when a company relocated to Bakersfield, it resulted in many other businesses booming, as well. Construction was certainly one of them. Plants and manufacturing warehouses, housing projects and road construction… the list went on.

Cam waved it off, though. "That has nothing to do with it. No matter how much a mechanic or a construction worker makes, you don't think about them when you hear the word 'success.' And you sure as shit don't think academic success about a mailman."

"That's what you were trying to say before, wasn't it?" Austin murmured. "We were talking about any kind of connection we might have, and you mentioned our jobs."

Cam nodded and wiped some sweat off his forehead. "It's what we have in common—menial jobs, so to speak. And you saw how that fucking prick went off on you and Tim when he learned about your degrees. Something's up with that. He didn't pick random dudes."

GALE NODDED AS Cam spoke; for once he was keeping his voice steady, and because he was talking, it was easier to remain in the present and not be sucked in completely by the past.

"It was the same theory Mr. Morris came to." Victor spoke of the FBI profiler who had been assigned to give answers to those who needed them. Cam wasn't one of them. Maybe the theories were true, but only one motherfucker could confirm.

"It doesn't fit with that insane bastard's real family members, though," Sean said, looking frustrated. "I'm working-class, out of a job at the moment, and he kept calling me Scott, some high school bully. But the real Scott... I read in an interview with him that he's a lawyer. Married, has kids, does charity—the whole shebang."

"Yeah," Victor agreed. "I was supposed to be his older brother, who is now raving about that lunatic in the papers. Says they were close and whatever, yet I was shot. Anyway, he—Fred, the older brother—is a successful spokesperson, fuckin' lobbyist, for some oil company."

Cam sighed and rolled his neck, closing his eyes for a beat. This could go on forever, and they'd never come to a conclusion. So, why bother? Psycho had lost his fucking marbles; let's leave it at that. Rhyme and reason wouldn't help him sleep better at night.

"He was intimidated by success."

Everyone turned to Chase, who had spoken up in his quiet, gruff voice. He had his knees drawn up, his forearms leaning on them, and his head was tilted back against the wall, eyes closed. He reminded Cam a little of himself with his rough exterior, though Chase was a couple years older. Holey jeans, biker boots, simple T-shirt, and a pair of Ray-Bans on top of his head.

Gale was pleasantly surprised—it was easy to tell—'cause Chase rarely talked. Even Cam and Austin, who were quiet, had nothing on Chase.

"Care to elaborate, Chase?" Gale asked encouragingly.

Chase opened his mouth without moving from his position

and kept his eyes closed as if he was napping. "They're all successful—that asshole's family members. It's pretty clear to me. I've read every interview, watched every news segment…" He shrugged with one shoulder. "He obviously felt like he'd been mistreated by these guys at some point in his life, but he was intimidated by their status. So, he took out his anger on ten innocent men who weren't all big shots. He could play boss with us. He wouldn't be able to do that with a lawyer, a CEO, a producer…"

It was quiet for a while before Tim said, "Remy, Stahl's little brother, works in a tattoo parlor. I don't see that as very successful."

Chase tensed up slightly at the mention of Remy, the name he'd been given in captivity, but answered without wavering. "He does that for kicks; it's his fucking hobby. He also runs a website—something with music, and the advertising makes him cash in like a king. Trust me, that fucker's loaded."

Chase had evidently done his research.

"Why would Stahl be intimidated by success, though?" Lance asked. "That's what I don't get."

Cam rolled his eyes, as there could be a million reasons and factors. "All it'd take is a case of Daddy issues. There're people all over the world who're fucked in the head 'cause of how they were raised." It was anyone's guess, and *that* was why Cam didn't give a fuck. "Maybe his pops told him that you're a fucking loser without an education or a good paying job." He shrugged.

Gale looked at the guys. "Well, that's certainly something to ponder, isn't it?"

Not really, Cam thought wryly. Weeks ago, they'd found out that Psycho's dad lived in some old folks' home and had Alzheimer's, so again, what did it matter? Were they gonna ask this old fuck who didn't know his own name how he'd raised his son?

Yeah, I don't fucking think so.

"Okay." Gale sat back and took a glance at her notepad. "Let's move on. What happened next?"

No one volunteered to answer.

WHEN PSYCHO SHOUTED, *"I said back off!" everyone heard it. Tim and Chase were already in the cell, and Cam and Austin got there a few seconds before Victor, Sean, and Lance did. Huddling near the doorway, they all saw the fucking Zippo lighter in Psycho's cuffed hands.*

"I thought you searched him." Chase slapped Tim's arm.

"For guns and keys," Tim snapped, clearly pissed he had missed the lighter Psycho must've had in one of his back pockets. And that goddamn lighter was functioning, the fairly large flame proof of that. An even bigger problem was that the gasoline Psycho had poured in the hallway outside the cells had slowly but surely seeped inside.

All it would take for this entire basement to go boom was dropping that lighter where he stood.

"You suicidal?" Cam asked him. He pointed at the wet floor. "If you drop that fucking lighter, you'll die, too. Not just us."

Psycho smiled. "By killing you, I will still do the world a favor. I will make a noble sacrifice." His smile became both wider and creepier. "Maybe this is how it was supposed to be all along. I'll go down as the hero who has taken out ten mediocre nobodies." Standing behind him, Austin placed a hand on Cam's hip, gently tugging him back from the doorway. Just a few inches, enough for Cam's back to touch Austin's chest. It was a silent request that said he didn't want Cam too close to the danger. Psycho went on with, *"My father will finally be proud."*

He looked so fucking pleased with himself that Cam shuddered. 'Cause this scumbag wasn't just insane—he was fucking delusional. Which had already been established, but now it reminded all the men that they were far from safe. Despite being restrained, Psycho held the power.

Victor tried to inch closer, but he didn't get far.

"Uh-uh-uh. One more step…" Psycho's warning was clear. He was fully prepared to drop that lighter and send them all to their deaths. *"In fact, why prolong this? I have nothing more to say."*

Before anyone could react, the lighter slipped from his hand.

SIXTEEN

AUSTIN PARKED NEXT to Cam's Camaro at the end of the parking row, killed the engine, unbuckled his seat belt, but didn't get out. Instead he grabbed his bottle of water and reached for the painkillers in the glove box, downed two, and sat back with a heavy sigh.

Taking off his sunglasses, he rubbed his tired eyes then slid the glasses up his nose again.

It was only Tuesday and this week was already killing him.

He'd gotten a lot done, but he understood Gale's reason for telling him to relax even more now. While it felt good to keep himself occupied, it made his mind spin. He suffered from furious headaches, and now he was in desperate need of a physical outlet to help with his anger issues.

Control was slowly making its return to Austin's life, though, so he was thankful for that. Because there was no other way to describe it. It was control. He'd taken control of his life. There was a plan, an agenda, things to do. He'd applied for all the papers needed, he'd talked to Angelo—his physical therapist—about what he could do to let off some steam, he'd found an apartment—as of twenty minutes ago—and he had started the process for Riley to change schools. But now, he was beyond beat. And he still had one more thing to do today: a session with Gale.

He already knew what it was about, which didn't make anything easier. At first, he didn't really think it was a big deal to miss one single group session, but when Gale told him what today's topic was going to be, he'd reluctantly made an individual appointment.

The last thing he wanted to do was to talk about how they broke free from that basement.

TIME SLOWED, MAKING every millisecond painfully clear. Austin didn't miss a single thing. He watched with horror in his widening eyes how the lighter was dropped and ignited the floor in a sea of fire.

Grabbing hold of Cam's arm, Austin ripped them backward. Someone shouted, "No!" Another one shouted, "Run!" In what felt like slow motion, Austin and Cam ran toward the stairs, quickly followed by the rest of the men.

Behind them, flames consumed the floor and began to lick the walls. Their kidnapper's evil laughs were replaced by ear-shattering screams. Everything was engulfed by the fire except for the concrete staircase. Hopefully, that would buy them a few seconds, because they still faced the problem of the door.

"Get ready to ram that door down!" Tim yelled.

They reached the small vestibule—much too small for seven men—and while someone closed the basement door behind them, Austin, Cam, Victor, and Chase charged for the door that led to freedom.

Pain ripped through Austin's body as his bad arm, shoulder; hell, his bad side made impact. But the door budged, so pain was pushed down. Beyond desperate, they all slammed their bodies toward the door, some of the guys getting mangled in the process. But Austin didn't give a shit, and he was one of the guys nearest the door. In his mind, he saw Riley. It made him fight harder. He had to see his baby girl again.

As smoke and heat rose, slithering into the vestibule under the basement's door, time and force became everything. The men didn't think about the future, although they were fueled by the thought of having one, and they didn't think about where they hurt.

Adrenaline surged through seven men, and two sayings became one. The first stated, "No man left behind," and the other stated, "Every man for himself." They contradicted each other, but it worked. While they shoved and used all the strength they could muster, not caring about who got smashed in the middle, they were still bound to one another. No one had any intention of leaving somebody else behind, but the main priority ensured they didn't give a rat's ass about bruises and broken bones.

Austin thought briefly about those two sayings and how the words he'd exchanged with Cam a few times summed it all up. Gun or no gun. Regardless of whether they got hurt, they would do their best to get free. But maybe it went a little further than that. Because to Austin, Cam was just a bit more important to get out than the others.

Blood, sweat, and tears mingled with the smoke that slowly filled the small space, but their efforts paid off. Just as Lance started saying something about choking from the smoke, the hinges on the door gave away.

"Yes!" Victor shouted hoarsely.

"Come on!" Chase barked out.

Gasping for air, Austin and Cam grabbed at each other, much like the others did, and ran for their lives, making sure they were all included. Blindly, they headed toward light. Freedom was the only thing on their minds, but they did register the wooden structure that surrounded them, much like the torture room. This place was about to go up in flames. The house was old, really damn old, and everything looked aged and about to crumble.

Passing closed rooms, heavily draped windows, and a filthy kitchen, at last they reached what had to be the door leading outside.

The cool night air met them as they emerged.

"Oh, God." Sean let out a breathless sob as they ran toward a barn about five hundred feet away.

"Don't stop!" Tim grabbed Sean by the arm and made sure they kept running.

To anybody else, it wasn't a "cool" night. It was dry, hot, and a thunderstorm could be heard in the distance—something very common for the Mojave Desert in the middle of summer. That was where Austin guessed they were. It had to be.

Nevertheless, the slightest breeze felt like an icy chill to the guys who had suffered months of stifled humidity in a basement.

The barn had seen better days; the front side was almost completely gone, wooden boards missing and rusty nails littering the ground. The doors being gone, too, left two gaping holes, one from the ground, one from the hay loft.

It was shelter, though, and all the men ran inside, just barely giving a crap about the nails and screws on the ground. They were all barefoot, and *several other clothing items were missing, as well. Austin stood in his torn sweats that clung to his hips, Cam wore his coveralls—the arms still tied around his narrow waist—Victor was only in boxer shorts and a work T-shirt, Sean wore holey jeans... everything was torn and threadbare.*

As the house they'd escaped was swallowed by flames, seven survivors stared blankly at the destruction while catching their breaths. Grime, blood—old and new—sweat, and some soot covered their features. Streaks from salty tears joined the mix, making trails down their cheeks.

"I... I can't..." Cam gasped and bent down to rest his hands on his thighs. He couldn't believe any of this, Austin knew. And Austin couldn't, either. He couldn't grasp the reality. They were free, but the knowledge wouldn't sink in.

Glancing around them, Austin took in the classic desert landscape. As far as he could see in the night, only the burning house and the barn stood taller than the small bushes, rock formations, and the occasional Joshua tree. Without knowing where in the desert they were, the guesses could pile up endlessly.

Austin wasn't a stranger to the desert, but when his father had taken him camping when he was younger, they stuck to trails and tourist spots, only venturing into the empty wilderness for shorter hikes. You did not want to get lost out here.

Temperatures could go to the extremes in both directions, depending on season and elevation.

"I suppose it's too risky to get that truck over there, huh?" Lance jerked his chin to the old Chevy that stood close to the house.

"Don't even think about it," Tim affirmed. "We don't even know where the keys are."

Just a moment later, the truck caught on fire, too.

AUSTIN TOOK A deep breath, his lungs expanding with the late-afternoon air. The windows were rolled down in his Mercedes, creating a nice cross-breeze, and the car stood in the shadow of a couple trees.

He reminded himself that he never had to go through that again.

Riley had always been an active girl, enjoying the outdoors and so on, but due to what Austin had been through, he'd actually denied her when she asked if she could get her own computer at Austin's new place. Partly, he thought she was too young to have her own, but it was mostly because he wanted to encourage her to go out and play with her friends instead of texting and PM-ing them—or whatever it was called these days.

For being called social networks, they sure involved a lot of time spent holed up alone.

He'd promised her a dog instead, which had certainly cushioned the blow of having to switch schools. Perhaps it was a dirty trick, but Austin couldn't care less about that. He'd take the responsibility. Hopefully, he'd return to work soon, too, and then he could always hire someone to take the dog out midday.

There was a lot of adjusting coming Austin's way, but he was ready. It couldn't be worse than other shit he'd had to adjust to.

WHEN DAWN APPROACHED, the men were sedate and silent in the barn.

Sitting on the ground, Cam and Austin leaned against each other for support and comfort. Sure, they could rest against the walls, but they preferred not to run into any snakes or worse. In this climate, there was no doubt what hid underneath rocks and wood.

"Do you guys see that over there?" Sean asked before yawning.

Tiredly following the man's gaze, Austin squinted and thought he saw a trail of dust. But it was too far away, so he couldn't be sure.

"Think it's a car?" Victor asked.

"I fuckin' hope so," Chase muttered. "We don't wanna be stuck here when the sun comes up."

They all knew what he was talking about. Throughout the night, the fire had raged on, and if that light hurt their eyes, the sun would blind them and scar them for life. Already, Austin could feel his eyes stinging with protective tears, and the sun was barely touching the horizon.

He hadn't thought about his reading glasses in a long time, but he supposed he'd get new ones soon. His vision wasn't far from 20/20, but he often got headaches from straining his eyes, so his glasses helped him. And now? Well, he knew if the sun did any damage, it might impair his vision.

People might think these men should be jumping for joy now that they were finally free. But how could they? Austin himself felt like a shell, and he was sure the others felt the same. He couldn't really muster any feelings other than dazed and tired. Jesus Christ, was he tired. Like the rest of them, he was also malnourished, in a severe amount of pain, and it wouldn't be long until dehydration kicked in, too. Not in this heat.

The air felt kind of fresh, though. He liked that.

"You okay?" Cam touched his scruffy cheek to get his attention.

Austin nodded automatically, eyes on the approaching trail of dust.

It was probably someone who had seen the fire. Maybe. Well, he hoped it was.

"You?" Austin asked back as an afterthought.

"Peachy."

As it turned out, it was a man and his son who drove the truck. They'd seen the smoke from the house fire and had decided to drive over to check it out.

They were shocked to see the seven men; the seven men were blank.

Austin and the others found out they were just outside Johannesburg, or Jo-burg as the two locals called it, and it was one of the many ghost towns in the area. Why it was called a ghost town when a group of people—no matter how small it was—still lived there, Austin didn't understand.

But that didn't matter.

Two strangers were about to take them back to Bakersfield.

The sun rose on the way.

The men covered their faces with their hands.

DIRECT SUNLIGHT AFTER months without it, combined with the desert dust, had definitely caused Austin some problems. One doctor told him it was the darkness in the basement that had impaired his vision, and another one said it was sudden sun exposure that had caused it. No matter the reason, he now needed his glasses—and shades for when the sun was out. Stupidly, he didn't follow the doctors' orders all the time, but he tried. He could still function without them, but it was only a matter of time before the headaches came, not to mention dryness and the mother of all itches.

Checking the time, he noticed the group session would end soon, and he hoped to get a minute alone with Cam before he had to drag his own ass up to Gale's office. Because these past days had been fucking exhausting, and he missed Cam. He missed him a lot.

On a few occasions, he'd thought about telling Gale about his new... *could it be called a relationship?*... whatever it was, with Cam, but he'd decided not to. At least not yet. It was so new, and it was a safe haven he wanted to keep to himself for now. Maybe if he'd considered it to be unhealthy to be with Cam, Austin would speak up, but he couldn't.

It wasn't like he had to see Cam every hour of the day. He didn't feel particularly clingy or needy; he didn't get anxious when Cam left the house or anything. He just wanted... he wanted them to be together. Spend their nights together, be closer than a phone call away, and have the same place to call home. He wasn't ready for it yet, and he had to think of Riley, too, but it was what he ultimately wanted—

Cam opened the passenger door and got in before Austin could finish his thought.

"Fuck, you scared me." Austin blew out a breath. Turning in his seat, he took in the mouthwatering sight he'd missed. "How did the session go?" He wanted to reach out, but this was the first time they were out in public since... well, since they'd fucked. Austin wasn't sure what was okay to do.

They were at the far end of the parking lot, though—several spots available between Cam's Camaro and the next car—so he supposed it was safe…

"It went," was all Cam said, and he wasn't struggling internally. He leaned over the console and the cup holders and pulled Austin in for a hard kiss. "You're in a suit," he mumbled, palming Austin's crotch.

"Christ," Austin hissed. Despite his shock, he bucked his hips into Cam's touch. It was all instinctual. "I—I thought I'd skip the beach bum look for when I looked at the apartment." He abandoned all words and deepened the kiss. There were fifteen minutes until his session with Gale; he was going to make the most of it. "Let me just roll up the windows." Now he wished there was such a thing as medical exemption for the tint laws in Cali; alas, there wasn't. It wouldn't be completely secluded, but the windows were still partially tinted.

"Did you get the place?" Cam asked huskily as Austin went for the fly on his jeans. "No, fuck that." He pushed Austin back and started unbuckling Austin's belt. Then he unzipped his fancy suit pants. "Now answer my fucking question."

"I, ah—" Austin groaned when Cam pulled out his semi-hard cock. "Shit. Yeah, I got it. Signed a six-month lease and paid the first month's rent—*ahh.*" Cam leaned down and swallowed him whole. "*Ohhh.*"

How many times in the past few days had he thought about this? Austin had lost count. Sliding off his shades, he placed them on the dashboard to see Cam better. Then he threaded his fingers through Cam's hair and just focused on his lover's amazing mouth.

"Suck me slowly," Austin murmured. By now, he was rock

hard and hitting the back of Cam's throat with each pass. "Fucking perfect." He groaned and guided their movements. His hips thrust upward, and he pushed past Cam's wet, soft lips, feeling his cock slide along Cam's tongue. "Damn," he moaned. "I could've used you in my showers." The fantasies didn't come close to the real thing.

"Oh, yeah?" Cam kissed and licked the length, reaching Austin's sac. He kissed and licked there, too. And sucked. "Don't hold out on me. Tell me what you've thought about."

It was pretty damn difficult to think, though. "Uh…" Austin's eyes were fixed on Cam's mouth. "About fucking you. I want to be inside you again." His head lolled back against the headrest as Cam sucked him in once more and hummed. "I can't stop thinking about you." He also wanted Cam to fuck him. In his morning showers, Austin had released in thick streams of come, a tight grip on his erection and fingers in his ass—all at the thought of Cam taking him. "I want you inside me, too," he admitted in a lust-filled voice. And this time, Cam moaned around him and sped up. He tightened his lips, which drove Austin to the brink of insanity.

It had hurt at first to finger himself, but fantasies about Cam doing it had made Austin love it. First one, while he made himself hard, then two as he stroked roughly toward a release, then three as he came against the shower wall.

When his body tensed up without warning, waves of heat washing through him, he barely got a word out before his climax took over. But Cam had obviously sensed it. While Austin rocked deeper into his mouth, Cam swallowed and kept sucking. His tongue swirled around the head, and his teeth grazed teasingly along the tight skin.

"Goddamn…" Having unconsciously held his breath, Austin started to pant. He slumped in his seat as Cam tucked him back into his boxer briefs and zipped up his pants. In an oddly tender gesture, he also grabbed Austin's hand and kissed it—and he noticed why.

It was the left ring finger he'd kissed. Austin shivered, warmth surging inside him. There was no ring there anymore. He'd taken it off when he'd woken up on Sunday morning, and now only a faint tan line reminded him of the woman who'd given him Riley.

Gently grasping Cam's chin, Austin tried to make him look up. "Look at me, baby."

"Not yet," Cam said, straightening in his seat. He adjusted his erection and stared at the brick building which they were parked in front of. Austin didn't pressure him, knowing eye contact wasn't always easy for him. "You're still coming over tonight?"

Austin nodded slowly even though Cam didn't face him. "If it's all right with you." He'd do anything to get inside Cam's head right now. Something was clearly on his mind.

Cam nodded jerkily and opened the car door. "More than all right. I'll see you later." Without another word, Cam left Austin's car and got into his own.

Unbeknownst to Austin, Cam had just realized that he was, in fact, in love.

It had clicked when he'd seen that ring finger bare.

And it was freaking him out just a bit.

SEVENTEEN

"I HAVE A suggestion for tonight," Austin said, clearing his throat. He threw the pizza crust into the box on the coffee table and shifted on the bed, facing Cam fully. The sheet around his hips parted a little, exposing his thighs.

"Sounds serious." Cam smirked and grabbed another slice of pizza. "Don't ruin shit now that I'm in a good mood."

Austin snorted a chuckle. "Yeah, you're as jolly as Santa." He shook his head, getting back on track. "Spend the night with me in your bedroom."

In the past two months, a lot had changed. For the better.

Austin liked his new two-bedroom apartment just five minutes away from Cam's house, Riley had made plenty of friends at her new school, things between Austin and Jade were civil, the house had finally been sold, the flashbacks and nightmares had gotten easier to deal with, Riley was in love with her new rat of a dog, Nacho—a black Chihuahua—and Austin was back to work.

He had routines. There were schedules. Sometimes it got hectic, but he made sure there was time to relax, too. He religiously went to all his sessions with Gale, and he'd found a workout regimen that made him feel better. It involved running, swimming, and kickboxing, all of which improved his health, both physically and mentally.

When Riley was with her mother in Delano, Austin barely left Cam's house, and they found plenty of time to see each other when Riley was with friends or had after-school activities. But he wanted more… God, he fucking *longed* for it.

It was last month that Cam had—during sex—mumbled, "I want it all with you." And it had triggered Austin's desires for the same to morph into demanding cravings. Sometimes, it was all he could think about.

He didn't want to hide his relationship with Cam. Although, hiding wasn't exactly right. It was just Riley. And Jade, but she didn't really count anymore, did she?

Austin had told his parents, which was actually a fond memory, at least in comparison to many others who'd "come out." There was no denying that he'd been nervous, mainly because he'd always been close to his mom and dad. If they didn't approve, it would hurt greatly.

He recalled the tense silence that followed after he admitted that he'd fallen for the man he'd been locked up with. Then his dad had broken the silence.

"YOU KNOW, SON, most men who hit their forties battle their little midlife crisis by buying a Porsche." Griffin gave his son a pointed look. *"That could work for you, too."*

Austin let out a quiet, shaky laugh. He was relieved. If this was the response, he considered himself lucky.

"Oh, honey." Maggie suddenly looked disapproving. *"If this is some phase, I hope there's no boy's heart out there you're going to crush."*

THIS DEFINITELY WASN'T a phase. Austin loved the man next to him beyond words, and now he was finally ready to move on. He wanted Riley to meet him, he wanted silly things like holding Cam's hand in public, and he wanted to make sure it was all heading somewhere.

As stated, he *liked* his apartment. He didn't love it. And he'd chosen it in Cam's neighborhood for only one reason. To be closer. The apartment was temporary. At least he hoped it was.

"No," Cam eventually said. "I'm not ready. The bedroom's too small—I'll f-feel suffocated."

"Have you even tried?" Austin shifted closer and cupped Cam's cheek. He didn't force Cam to look him in the eye, but he needed contact. "Gale thinks you should try."

"Fuck what she says," Cam spat out, throwing his pizza slice into the box on the table. "You know, I don't see why it fucking matters—"

"It matters," Austin insisted quietly. Pushing Cam back against the bed, Austin moved over him, hovering closely. Only a sheet separated their naked bodies. It was Saturday, and their favorite pastime was to fuck each other like crazy and just lounge around. No need for clothes then. "It matters if we want more."

Cam looked up at him strangely. "More?" He scooted up the bed, Austin following, and seemed willing to hear him out. "More what?" There was cautious hope in his eyes.

"Of us," Austin admitted. It was about damn time to lay it all out there. "Let me start by saying that I don't want to renew my lease in four months." He thought that would give them a good amount of time to get used to *more*.

There was only the matter of making things official. Austin had already spoken to Cam's parents on the phone, and while they didn't know his true label, they weren't stupid. Landon and Jules had figured out the obvious without confirmation. Gale probably had her guesses. His parents knew and wanted to meet Cam.

Yeah, Austin was fucking nervous about it, but he had promised himself not to be content with content anymore. He wanted to take risks in order to get what he yearned for. He wanted to come clean to Riley about the man she only knew as Dad's friend. Not that they'd met yet, but it had been discussed. With both of them. Cam wanted to meet her, and Riley wanted to meet Dad's friend who had a cool dog named Bourbon Mulligan.

"You—" Cam broke off, his mind spinning.

"I promise I won't push you," Austin murmured. "But will you at least think about it?" He paused, reminding himself that Cam wasn't made out of glass. He could handle the truth. After all, Austin wasn't the only one who made progress each day. It was clear that Cam loved his work, and he was putting in many hours at Landon's garage. At home, he was at ease. He liked his space, but he didn't need to have all the lights on anymore. He hadn't had a cigarette indoors in weeks, and… things were just better. "I want there to be a bedroom for privacy," he continued quietly. "We'd need it if… if we weren't alone in the house." He raised a brow.

"Oh." Cam swallowed. "You want—you want more. That way." He hesitated. "What about Riley?"

"I want you to meet her." He lowered his face and kissed Cam lightly. "As my partner. As someone I want in my life permanently."

At last, Austin didn't have a single doubt about his feelings and intentions.

There was a time everything had confused him, but even then, he hadn't been able to stay away.

"I KNEW I'D find you here," Austin chuckled, slowly limping toward Cam who was standing just outside the ambulance bay smoking a cigarette. Austin wondered who he'd bribed to be allowed here, and it wasn't the first time. But they all did everything they could to avoid the press.

Eight days ago when they'd returned to Bakersfield, Austin wasn't the only one who had collapsed from sheer exhaustion. With news crews camping outside the hospital, the men had been blissfully unaware and sedated. Bullets had been removed, bones had been reset, countless tests had been done, blood had been given, and nutrition was being pumped into them intravenously.

Cam grunted and took a deep drag from his smoke.

They were both wearing protective sunglasses that made them look like freaks, but they were needed. Especially in broad daylight with the sun directly overhead.

"My gums still hurt." Cam ran the tip of his tongue over his front teeth. They felt smooth and clean now, but it was still painful to brush them.

Austin knew the feeling. "Are you nervous?" he wondered as he reached Cam. It felt better now—to be close to his former cellmate. For more than one reason, he was happy to be out of his hospital gown. Now, he tucked his hands into the front pocket of his sweatshirt; it was all he could do before his hands did something else. Something he couldn't understand or explain.

"Too many people up there." Cam shrugged one shoulder. "You okay?" He eyed Austin behind his shades.

"Under the circumstances," he answered vaguely.

Truth was, he was far from okay. He felt like a ticking time bomb.

Having Riley update him on the news around the world by reading the paper to him was one thing. It was a whole other matter to listen to Jade go on and on about the police investigation and what had happened in Bakersfield while Austin and the others had been missing. Anger kept building up inside him, and he didn't know what to do with it.

Five months and three days. That was how long he'd been in that basement.

"Don't bullshit me." Cam took a final pull from the cigarette before stubbing it out under his shoe. "Not me, Austin." He shoved the butt down in his pack, then pocketed it. "Talk. What's up?" He placed a hand on Austin's shoulder.

Austin swallowed, feeling awkward and out of place. "Nothing's up. I'm all right."

"Yeah." Cam's mouth formed a small smile. "I can see that."

"His name was Ben," Austin blurted out. He exhaled harshly and dragged a hand over his clean-shaven face. "Ben Stahl. That—that was his name." And he, that psychotic madman, had been counted as one of the victims. In the papers, he had been reported missing around the same time Cam was. His mother had gone to the police, stating that she hadn't heard from her son in days. Like the rest of the guys, Ben Stahl had had his fifteen minutes of fame while the police searched for clues. "They've done pieces on him—interviews with his family, honorable shit about what a kind man he is... was."

"I know." Cam had heard about it, too.

"It pisses me off," Austin whispered, looking down. "I'm so fucking angry, Cam."

"Whoa, dude. Did you just drop the f-bomb?"

Austin smiled weakly.

Cam sighed and stepped closer, his other hand touching Austin's elbow. And Austin felt how the fingers curled to fit the shape of him. He closed his eyes, battling an indescribable yearning inside of him. He didn't get it. He didn't understand a thing of what was going on.

"We'll make sure everyone finds out he's not so innocent," Cam reasoned and closed the distance between them. He hugged Austin to him, who in turn hugged Cam back fiercely. "There's no way we'll let the world think he's a victim, all right?"

Austin nodded into Cam's neck, allowing himself a moment where he didn't even try to be strong. Sooner or later, he would return to Jade and Riley, and he would put on a mask. He'd be father of the year and husband of the... well, he was decent, anyway.

Too soon, Cam was angling away from Austin, starting with his hips and then loosening his arms around him. Austin took that as a cue to *man up and move away.*

"*Sorry,*" *he muttered, averting his eyes.*

"*Don't mention it.*" *Cam's voice was oddly husky.*

A LOT HAD changed. A lot had been explained. Almost every truth had come out.

It was time for the last of Austin's. "I want you to meet her as the man I love."

He definitely wasn't expecting anything in return, and he had a feeling Cam needed a minute or two to let this settle, so Austin stopped talking for now and just focused on the beautiful body beneath him. He kissed his way down to the cock he'd had inside him countless times since the first time a couple months ago. He sure as hell never thought he'd become addicted to a cock.

"Austin…" Cam mumbled.

Austin hummed and sucked Cam's cock into his mouth, feeling it hardening with each stroke. They'd had sex this morning, Austin being the top, and now he wanted it the other way around. Because Cam as a lover… Christ, he was intense. He was ferocious, rough, yet focused on Austin's reactions and needs.

The minute Cam was done thinking, their roles reversed. Austin ended up on his back and watched as Cam's dominant side surged forward. *Damn sexy.* Reaching for the lube on the table, Cam returned to Austin, who spread his legs and pulled his knees up like a wanton slut.

"I need to fuck you," Cam muttered into Austin's neck. His

long fingers soaked Austin's hole and pushed inside, immediately finding his prostate.

"Oh, Jesus." The level of pleasure always blew Austin's mind. He fisted the sheets and watched helplessly as his dick thickened and grew longer without even being touched. Cam kept rubbing that spot inside him with the pads of his fingers until Austin was panting and bucking his hips. "Please, Cam," he gritted out. "*Fuck me.*"

Cam slowly pulled out his fingers, then lubed up his hard cock. About a month back, they'd gotten tested, and there was no better feeling than fucking raw. It had only been a formality, an end to all the tests they'd gone through, but the results gave them the chance to feel *everything* now. Supporting himself on one hand next to Austin's head, Cam guided his cock to Austin's ass and filled him in one thrust.

"Fuck," Cam exhaled harshly, dropping his forehead to Austin's collarbone. They were still for several heartbeats. And when Cam began to move, Austin was even more helpless than before. With their foreheads touching, Cam shoved his cock in and out of Austin's tight ass, and for once, Cam maintained eye contact. His silver eyes darkened with lust, and Austin found the gaze fucking scorching.

Cam slid his fingers into Austin's hair, fisting it, and angled them for a deep kiss. He spoke quietly with their warm lips touching and the tips of their tongues teasing. "I love you." He thrust in harder and groaned. "I love y-you so fucking much, Austin."

Austin hissed and pushed back, his face contorted in extreme pleasure and relief. "God, I love you." The burn Cam's cock caused only intensified everything that was amazing, and to add love to that mixture proved to be almost too much for Austin. Grabbing Cam's face, he pulled him down and kissed him hungrily. "Make me lose it."

"I will." Cam sat up slightly and placed Austin's left leg on his shoulder. Then they both watched as his slicked-up cock disappeared into Austin's ass. "Stroke yourself," he commanded huskily. "Stroke that thick cock—let me watch you."

"Cam," Austin grunted. He fisted his aching cock and stroked it to match Cam's pace. "I need more."

Cam smirked faintly, a bead of sweat trickling down his chest. "I know what you need."

After several minutes of hard fucking, Cam replaced his cock with his fingers. At first, Austin started to protest; he wanted that cock inside him, but when his prostate was being massaged again, he shut his mouth. His head swam, the ecstasy assaulting him from every angle.

"You're so close, baby," Cam murmured.

Austin nodded minutely, his eyes locked on Cam's cock. They were both stroking harder and tighter with every second that passed. Perspiration made their bodies glisten. Every straining muscle showed. *Oh, yes, yes, yes.* Austin let out a low moan as his insides coiled up.

When Cam applied pressure to Austin's prostate again, he lost it completely. His back arching, Austin gasped out a curse as his cock pulsed out streams of come. At the same time, Cam's orgasm hit, too. Moans and groans mingled, and they both released onto Austin's body.

Despite being physically healthier than ever before, Austin was exhausted. Right now, the only thing he wanted was to feel Cam pressed up against him and relax. Cam luckily had similar plans, and after they cleaned off, they snuck under the sheets and just enjoyed each others' bodies.

"I'll try," Cam said after a while as he lazily traced his fingers along Austin's spine. "The bedroom thing—I'll try."

Austin smiled and kissed Cam on the forehead. "We can always have the door open when we sleep. And if it doesn't work… we can buy a pull-out couch for the living room." That way, they could have their privacy in the bedroom, and then when it was time to sleep, Cam could do what felt best.

Three times in the past two months, Austin had accidentally startled Cam awake, which had led to him attacking Austin. For those reasons, he knew it was good they still had time to adjust.

He didn't want to imagine someone else waking Cam up and receiving the same treatment. Austin could handle it; he understood it and had a way of calming Cam down quickly. But Riley? Austin would never risk it. However, if Cam at least slept in the bedroom, Austin could tell Riley to never disturb Cam.

"I like this," Cam whispered, averting his gaze to Austin's shoulder. "Um, when you talk like—I like when you say things as if you live here. I like it."

Even though Cam had just said he liked it, Austin suddenly felt like a fucking idiot. His thoughts were way ahead. Sure, when you had children you needed to plan ahead, but he'd barely started to let Cam in on those thoughts.

"No rush," Austin promised. "We have time. And if you're not ready in four months—"

"Why are you backtracking?" Cam's eyes slid to Austin's, and he scowled. "Don't be an idiot. I don't like idiots." He said it so matter-of-factly that Austin wanted to smile. "Just 'cause we haven't talked a lot about this doesn't mean we haven't been heading in this direction for a long time now."

Cam was right. From the first night they'd been intimate, they had been devoted to each other without a single word uttered about it.

"I barely use the second bedroom," Cam said cautiously. "I mean, if Riley likes me…"

"She will love you." Austin's chest expanded. A million thoughts rushed through him, but first and foremost, it was the relief that made him feel damn near giddy. He could never forget when Riley said she had no desire to watch Mom and Dad meet others, but Austin remained hopeful. She was handling the divorce better now, and because Austin and Jade made sure to put Riley first without spoiling her, Austin was confident that she would come around.

"You can't know that." Cam glared and lay back, facing the ceiling. "I'm no good with kids. I don't know any kids. I don't have any social skills."

"With Riley, you won't need any," Austin reasoned. "She's easy to please. And not to make her sound like a materialistic brat, but you have a cute dog and a pool; she will love you." Even in late October, it was in the higher eighties, and they didn't exactly have a pool at their apartment.

"You gonna bring the rat over, too?" Cam had met Nacho once when Austin had taken him for a walk, and while Bourbon thought the little thing was a cool toy, Cam wasn't impressed. Neither was Austin, but it was what it was. "I'll sit on him, and then Riley will run away screaming." He threw an arm over his face. "Fuck."

Austin couldn't help it; he laughed. He laughed *hard*.

EIGHTEEN

A WEEK LATER, Cam was under Austin's command. It was a hot Saturday afternoon, and that was good. It meant Riley could use the pool.

Cam figured he needed all the help he could get, 'cause he was a fucking wreck. Which was why Austin was in charge. He handled that shit better than Cam.

Cam liked it, though. He wasn't being coddled; sometimes Austin pushed Cam, but he didn't pressure. There was a difference. He knew Cam's limits, and if anything, he made Cam feel stronger and more confident.

To make things easier today, Cam and Austin had invited their parents and Landon and Jules, too, but Cam wasn't sure that was a good thing. Now he had to impress Austin's folks, too, and Cam just didn't do that. He didn't impress people. He didn't suck up or mince words. Instead he fumbled awkwardly, had a knack for coming off as hostile, and he fidgeted.

The five minutes their families had met at the hospital right after the kidnapping wasn't enough for this to be a "nice to see you again" kind of scene. This was a "nice to meet you" occasion. Without beeping hospital machines, drugs, IVs, sluggish minds, and distress.

Much to Cam's relief, Jules and Landon were first to arrive.

"You look like you're about to shit your pants, little brother." Landon smirked.

"They're shorts, dickwad. And fuck you." Cam looked down at his board shorts, then looked at Jules. "Shouldn't you be at a hospital somewhere?" She was about to pop. Her belly was fucking huge, and there were two in there.

"You Nash boys always say the sweetest things," Jules said dryly. "Now, let me in. I need to sit down."

Cam moved out of the way just as Austin joined them in the hallway. "Right. This is Austin. Austin, my brother Landon, and Jules, my sister-in-law."

They were dressed pretty much the same—in board shorts and T-shirts—but Cam was sure Austin looked like a model while Cam came off as a homeless surfer. There was a handsome smile on Austin's face, his hazel eyes crinkling in the corners behind his glasses, a few strands of silver in his light brown hair, and he had a body that made Cam's dick perk up.

"It's nice to finally meet you—*officially*," Austin said, shaking Jules's hand. Like a suave bastard, he even kissed the top of it, which made Jules blush. She never fucking blushed.

"Oh, you too." Jules giggled like some schoolgirl. Landon and

Cam exchanged a look; the older Nash was slightly peeved, and the younger was amused. Austin probably shouldn't bring out Landon's possessive side. "He's so handsome, Cam."

"Very funny," Landon said gruffly and stepped forward. He shook Austin's hand, too, with unnecessary force, but Austin didn't seem to notice. The two men had the same build and height; they were even the same age. "So, you're with my little brother now, huh?"

"I am." Austin nodded and motioned for Jules to go to the patio. "And you should put your feet up." Of course, Austin had experience with pregnant women. "Anything you want to drink? Cam has stocked up on decaf iced tea."

"That sounds perfect." Jules was beaming. "Cam, don't let this one go." That said, she waddled toward the patio.

Landon grunted and followed.

"I'm not sure that was smart." Cam's mouth slanted up in a lazy smile. "Now you don't have my brother on your side."

Austin didn't appear threatened. "I have a feeling the way into Landon's good graces is by earning Jules's approval."

Damn. He was probably right. "Well, you have that and more," Cam huffed. "All right, gimme somethin' to do."

"You can bring Jules her iced tea." Austin squeezed Cam's ass, kissed him chastely, and returned to the kitchen. "And I suppose my parents will be here with Riley any minute," he called over his shoulder.

Cam muttered a few curses and followed him to the kitchen, where he knew Austin was about to call Jade. Maybe not the most opportune moment, but it gave Austin a reason to cut the call short if needed.

"Wish me luck," Austin drawled.

Cam snickered, grabbed a tray, and loaded it up with the pitcher of iced tea from the fridge, a couple beers, and a glass, then headed to the patio where Bourbon was jumping in and out of the pool. He could swim just fine, but he didn't like it. He did, however, love to cool off. So, he'd jump in a couple times, then go lie down in the shade with his bowl of water and whatever dog bone Cam had given him.

"You nervous?" Landon asked, nodding in thanks for the beer.

Cam shrugged and focused on the iced tea, never wanting to admit weaknesses.

"She'll adore you," Jules said confidently. "Austin's parents will, too."

"You've never even met them," Cam pointed out and slid a glass of iced tea toward her. He knew, with his luck, he'd end up killing Nacho.

Not wanting to hear more reassurances, Cam popped the cap on his beer and went back inside. He could hear Austin on the phone.

"No, Jade, I'm not trying to be funny," he was saying, and Cam caught his eye-roll just as he reentered the kitchen. "I wanted to call and tell you before Riley had the chance." There was a pause while Jade did the talking, and Cam raised an eyebrow, silently asking how it was going. Austin threw him a look of frustration in return, but there was a pinch of amusement there, too. "She thinks I'm kidding," he said, holding the phone away.

"Now she's berating me for my poor sense of humor."

Cam snorted and hopped up to sit on the kitchen counter. "Tell her I'm willing to send evidence." That was a joke. He tugged Austin to him and dropped a sensual kiss on his neck. Now that Austin was working again, he was always clean-shaven, and he smelled of an aftershave that made Cam's mouth water.

"Yes, I'm listening to you." Austin was speaking to Jade, but his focus was on Cam's mouth. And then Cam's hand on Austin's cock. "Uh-huh. Yeah, keep going—what?" Cam stifled a laugh. "No, no—I just... fuck. Listen, I told you what I wanted to tell you. Cam and I aren't just friends, and he's meeting Riley today. My parents are coming over, too." Jade said something, to which Austin grinned. "Believe what you want, Jade—"

Frustrated, Cam grabbed the phone out of instinct and blurted out the first words that came to mind. "The sooner you believe him, the sooner I can get him off the phone and suck his—"

"Cam!" Austin snatched the phone away, looking stunned, furious, *and* like he was ready to laugh his ass off—all at once. "Jesus Christ." He blew out a breath and pinched the bridge of his nose. "Jade?" He placed the phone by his ear, then sighed. "She hung up."

Cam tried to hide the fact he felt bad—hell, worse than that. He felt like shit.

"That was so fucking juvenile," Austin said, though not angrily or anything. That confused Cam, and when he chanced a glance at Austin's face, he saw mirth in his eyes. *Oh, thank fuck.* "Next time we're alone together..." He grabbed Cam's jaw. "You will make it up to me. Understand?"

Hell yeah, Cam understood. "Yes, sir." He saluted Austin.

Austin smirked like the sexy motherfucker he was, but the spell was broken when the doorbell rang.

Cam paled as he could hear Riley outside. Fuckin' kitchen window was open.

"Hey, none of that." Austin's eyes softened, and he kissed the spot between Cam's brows. "It'll be fine. Come on."

Griffin and Maggie Huntley were definitely Austin's parents. Griffin was basically an older version, but with much lighter features and more gray in his hair. Tall, solid, and with a polite smile on his face. Maggie was short, looked kind, had darker hair, and the same hazel eyes that Austin had.

When Cam saw the logo on the chest pocket of Griffin's short-sleeved shirt, he exchanged a quick look of wry amusement with Austin, who could read his mind at that point. If it weren't for the sweats with Griffin's construction business's logo on them that Austin had worn the day he was kidnapped, their lives would probably look a lot different now.

"Hi, Dad!" Riley bounced forward with Nacho in her arms and hugged Austin's middle.

"Hey, baby girl." Austin kissed the top of her head while Cam just watched.

Riley was… she was fucking cute. The brief time he'd seen her at the hospital right after they'd been saved, he hadn't really thought about it. And she looked more like Austin than Cam had originally thought. Her eyes were a little greener than brown, and her long hair was wavier, but it was Austin's coloring. There was a lot of Jade in her, too, and even some Maggie.

She dressed like a tomboy in denim shorts, All Stars sneakers, and a well-worn T-shirt that looked too big for her lanky frame, but Cam had seen plenty of photos of her. He knew she liked all things girl, too.

"I want you to meet Cam." Austin smiled at his girl and ushered her forward.

They'd agreed that Austin would take Riley aside later today and tell her everything, so for now, it was just Cam. No explanation. No title. Which he had to admit he preferred for the official meeting. Cam already felt nervous as it was. No need to add more pressure.

"Hello. I'm Riley Huntley," Riley said shyly, keeping close to Austin. "Daddy's shown me pictures of Bourbon. And this is Nacho." She pointed to the rat-sized dog in her arms.

Cam smiled nervously and barely resisted fidgeting. "It's good to meet you, Riley." He cleared his throat and looked toward the patio. "Bourbon's probably in the backyard if you wanna meet him. Uh, there's a pool, too—you know, if you wanna swim or whatever."

"Oh, *yes*. Dad told me." Riley nodded furiously. "Can I go change now?" She looked up at Austin, who chuckled.

"I'll take her," Maggie offered, stepping forward. She extended her hand to Cam. "It's so good to see you again, Cam."

"You too, Mrs. Huntley." Cam nodded. "The bathroom is just down the hall. Or here, I guess." He pointed to the half-bath next to him. "It's not very big, though."

"Thank you. And it's Maggie." She winked. "Come on,

sweetie." She began to usher Riley down the hall. "Best we get Nacho ready, too."

"They insisted on giving that little rodent a life jacket," Griffin said wryly, and he was the last to greet Cam. "My boy's told me a lot about you. I hear you're good with cars."

"Yeah." Cam shook his hand. "I mean, uh, yes. Yes, sir. Fuck." He let out a frustrated breath.

Griffin barked out a laugh and slapped Austin on the back. "I approve, son." He smirked, much like Austin. "Now, I was told there was beer. Mags is driving."

Austin shook his head, amused. "Go out on the patio; I'll bring some."

When it was just the two of them left in the hall, Cam sagged against the wall and tugged at his hair. "That was fucking brutal."

"No." Austin disagreed. "We know what brutal is, and this wasn't it." He had a point. "I want you to relax and just be yourself now. My parents aren't fancy people, so stop acting like it."

Cam nodded grudgingly and allowed Austin to drag him away from the hall.

Now they were just waiting for Jonathan and Lily, Cam's folks.

THIS WAS WHAT Austin wanted.

Now, an hour or so later, the Nashes and the Huntleys had meshed together perfectly. Griffin and Jonathan were manning the grill, talking about the economy. Maggie, Lily, and Jules were at the table, and the unborn twins were the popular subject there.

As suspected, Jonathan and Lily had already had an idea about Austin and Cam, and they were very accepting.

Meanwhile, Cam, Austin, and Landon were in the pool with Riley and two dogs. The kidney-shaped pool was only about twelve feet wide and twenty feet long, but it was plenty for a family of three, and deep enough in the middle for the water to reach Riley's chest, and she was on her toes then.

"See?" Riley shouted. "Nacho can swim!"

"With a life jacket, yeah," Austin laughed, swimming over to her. "Get ready, baby girl." Picking her up, he threw her over to where Cam was helping Bourbon out of the pool.

"Incoming!" Riley squealed.

Bourbon barked and wagged his tail, jumping in again, to which Cam chuckled and groaned. The only thing that scratched up your skin more than a dog was a wet dog.

"Jules, we gotta get one of these!" Landon had evidently fallen for Nacho.

"You're paying for that shit, Austin," Cam chuckled darkly. "Come here, sweetheart." It was his turn to pick up Riley, and she was thoroughly enjoying being thrown around. "Splash as much as you can."

She giggled as he raised her in the air. "I will."

Not holding back, Cam threw a laughing and flailing Riley toward Austin, who ducked underwater right as she hit the surface.

Austin resurfaced laughing and coughing with Riley clinging

to him and trying to push him under again. "Cheater, Dad!"

"I think the steaks are done now," Jonathan said casually.

"IT'S GOOD SEEING you more relaxed," Austin murmured, coming up behind Cam in the kitchen. Everyone else was outside enjoying the last of the sun and just talking. "It's going well, isn't it?" He kissed Cam's neck.

Dinner was over, and now it was coffee, more beer, sodas, ice cream, and desserts coming up.

"I haven't killed Nacho yet, so I suppose it's all good. For now." Cam turned around and placed his hands on Austin's hips. "Your mom's a fucking riot, by the way."

Austin hummed and claimed Cam's mouth with his. He had no interest in talking about his mother. Now that they were officially a couple with their families aware and accepting, it was difficult to stick to innocent touches. Austin couldn't honestly call himself big on public displays on affection, but there was a difference between hand-holding and chaste kisses, and ass-groping and teenage-like make-outs. He definitely wanted the aforementioned.

"Um." That wasn't Cam or Austin.

Breaking away, Austin looked over his shoulder and cursed internally at the sight of Riley in the doorway.

She looked like she'd been caught with her hand in the cookie jar, and she was blushing profusely.

"Fuck," Cam whispered, scrubbing his hands over his face.

"Talk to her."

Austin cleared his throat, his heart suddenly pounding, and turned to his daughter. "Uh, let's go find a quiet place." Guiding Riley past the living room and down the hall, he opened the door to Cam's second bedroom, which was pretty empty aside from some gym equipment.

Maybe this was why Austin hadn't been nervous about meeting Cam's family. He'd been waiting for this instead—telling his daughter that he was in a relationship so quickly after separating from Riley's mother.

Austin sat down on a chair next to a rack of dumbbells. "I have something to tell you."

Riley nodded, still avoiding his gaze, and let out a breath. "Do I need a stiff drink for this?" Austin was fairly certain he dropped his jaw at that, but Riley just waved him off. "I heard Landon say that to Jules when they talked about saving money for the twins' college. And Pops 'splained it to me."

"I, uh… I see." Austin wasn't sure he liked how adult she sounded. She was supposed to be his baby girl forever. "Well, what you saw in the kitchen—"

"You were kissing Cam," she stated.

"Right." He nodded and phrased his words carefully. "I care about him very much—"

Riley gave him a funny look and cut him off—*again*, to Austin's frustration. This was already difficult enough as it was. "I'm ten, Dad. I know that friends don't kiss like you kissed." She scowled and put her hands on her hips. "Are you peoples like Uncle Derek now?"

"People," he corrected automatically as his mind spun.

The question had thrown him off, and he tried to understand where Riley's thoughts were. Though, at the mention of his cousin who was gay, it didn't take too long to catch up, and he was suddenly thankful for Derek. Not to mention his parents' strict acceptance of everyone. Since Derek lived on the East Coast, Riley didn't see him very often, but she had met him. And his partner.

"Peoples makes more sense. It's plural of people," Riley retorted indignantly. "One people, many peoples. One person, many persons." Austin didn't have the heart to correct her; she was being too cute. "But are you? Are you and Cam peoples like Uncle Derek?"

He took a breath and released it. "I suppose you could say that," he answered slowly and carefully. "We're together, if that's what you mean."

"That's what I mean." She chewed on her lip. "Is that why you divorced Mom?"

"No," Austin said quickly. "Remember how Mom and I told you that grown-ups sometimes drift apart?"

"Yeah, I remember," she said, having heard it too many times. "Mom said you started having problems years ago." Well, that was one way of putting it. No need to go into semantics. "But, I mean... did you have problems 'cause you like boys?"

Austin let out a shaky laugh. "No, baby girl. That's not why we had problems."

He didn't feel like adding a long rant about the fact that he wasn't strictly attracted to one gender, but attraction was one thing. Cam was still the first man Austin felt drawn toward to the point of complete surrender. He had admired men in the past and thought nothing of it, but with Cam it was so different.

"So… what do you think about all this?" He tilted his head, trying to read Riley's face. "Cam's nice, isn't he?" He *needed* his daughter to approve of Cam.

"He's cool." She shrugged, then scrunched her nose. "He cusses a *lot*," she giggled, and Austin grinned.

"Yeah, it takes some getting used to, doesn't it?" he chuckled. "But today he was nervous. He curses more then."

"Why was he nervous?"

"Because he wants you to like him," he replied softly. "He knows how important you are to me—that you're number one—so that means your opinion of him matters." He'd added the number-one part because he wanted Riley to understand that she wasn't being replaced. He'd read online that many children feared neglect when their divorced parents met new partners.

"Do you love him?" Riley asked. "Is he gonna move in with us? Did he ask you to be his boyfriend? Or did you ask him?" She was on a roll now. "Are you gonna have a baby—" She stopped short at that one. "How would that even *work*?"

Austin opened his mouth then closed it again. *Holy hell.* The girl was inquisitive. "How about this—" he paused, racking his brain "—we're going to take this slow. Yes, I love him. No, he's not going to move in with us, but…" He hesitated. "One day," *soon, he hoped,* "if this works out, we might move in with him. Here. His house is better than our apartment, right?" Riley quickly glanced out the window toward the pool, and Austin had her answer. "You'd get your own room, of course. This one, actually.

We'd redecorate it for you. It was Cam's suggestion." One point for Cam. "But, Riley, not yet. Right now, we'll focus on getting to know each other. For instance, I've told Cam that you're awesome at soccer. He'd love to come to your next game."

"He can do that." She grinned, proud of herself.

Austin was beyond relieved. "Do you understand what I'm saying, though? We'll start off slow. Maybe we can have movie nights, go to your games, have dinners together, take Bourbon and Nacho to the park, perhaps sleep over here sometimes…"

"I understand the conspect of slow, Dad." She rolled her eyes. "I'm ten."

Austin laughed through his nose and shook his head. "Concept, baby girl. And I know you understand; I just want to make sure you don't think everything is going to change overnight. Are you okay with all this?"

"*Yes*," she replied, sounding aggravated. "Mom's already told me that she's getting ready to start dating again or whatever. Can I have ice cream now?"

She can have all the ice cream in the world.

When Austin and Riley returned to the patio, the atmosphere was stilted and uncomfortable. Austin noticed how tense Cam was, so he concluded that they were all basically waiting for a result of the Dad and Daughter talk. The way Riley bounced over to the ice cream made Maggie and Lily look hopeful, and Austin's reassuring smile put the rest at ease.

"You can relax," Austin said quietly, sitting down next to Cam, whose shoulders visibly sagged with relief. "Everything went well." He grabbed Cam's hand and kissed it before threading their fingers together.

That was that.

For the rest of the evening, the two families continued to get to know each other, and whenever Austin and Cam even touched each other, Riley would giggle, roll her eyes, and turn red in the face.

LATER THAT NIGHT when everyone had gone home, Austin and Cam stepped into the shower together in silence. Both were thinking about how well it had gone today, and while Austin was already planning a day he could spend with both Riley and Cam, Cam was simply enjoying the moment.

The reason Austin felt bold enough to think ahead was because Cam had told him earlier that they should go out and buy a pull-out couch for the living room.

It had felt like the proverbial green light. Cam was ready to try, and he wanted Riley comfortable when she visited. So, the living room would become a living room again, and Cam's bedroom would now belong to two men. When Austin spent the night, anyway.

"No, let me." Cam grabbed the bodywash from Austin. "I was gonna make things up to you, remember?"

Austin chuckled tiredly. "I was mostly joking, you know."

"Your dick wasn't." Cam smirked. "Now, turn around."

Austin turned around, enjoying the hot water cascading down his naked body, then groaned in pleasure when Cam began to massage his shoulders, using bodywash instead of lotion.

"Do you think her room's gonna be all pink and bubblegum-y?" Cam asked after a minute. "'Cause I don't know if I can handle that shit."

Austin grinned lazily to himself and dropped his chin to his chest. "I think her favorite color right now is yellow, but it changes."

The original plan had been for Austin and Riley to go home to their apartment tonight, but now there was a new agenda. Riley was excited at the prospect of decorating her own room, even if it wouldn't be fully hers just yet. Regardless, she had tricked Nana and Pops into driving her around tomorrow to check color samples for the walls in Cam's second bedroom. So, she was spending another night with them.

"I can deal with yellow," Cam murmured, and that ended the subject.

Cam rubbed Austin's shoulders and upper back in firm and sensual strokes. His fingers kneaded the flesh, eliciting quiet groans from Austin. Then farther down his spine. When Cam told him to put his hands on the tiled wall and spread his legs, Austin did. He supported himself while Cam got down on his knees.

"Damn," Austin exhaled. Cam was kneading his thighs, the hot water washing away the suds quickly. It felt so fucking good. There was anticipation in the air, too. The closer Cam's fingers got to his ass, the harder his cock grew. Soon he felt those long fingers spreading his cheeks, still massaging and washing, but it was Cam's mouth that made him moan. "Jesus Christ..." His thighs shook with tension as Cam teased his hole with his tongue and fingers.

At the same time, Cam was fingering his own ass, too. Reaching down, Austin began to stroke himself just as the tip of Cam's tongue entered him. It was soft, wet, and goddamn erotic.

Cam hummed and fucked him slowly with his tongue. Deep wasn't deep enough, hard wasn't hard enough; Austin grew frustrated with greed and started to push back.

"I think you're ready," Cam laughed quietly and withdrew. Standing up, he switched places with Austin and gave him a look over his shoulder. "There's lube on the counter."

Austin frowned and pushed away the shower curtain; sure enough, there was a bottle of lube. He grabbed it and raised a brow at Cam. "You planned this?" They didn't exactly have a bottle of lube in every room of the house.

"You bet I did," Cam said, facing the wall. "I have needs, and when you're all riled up, you give it to me hard. I'm ready."

Austin had expected it to be the other way around tonight, but Cam's words surged through him like an aphrodisiac. All he wanted now was to slam his cock inside Cam's ass. So, that's what he did after lubing up and nudging Cam's legs apart.

"Fuck," Cam choked out.

"Hard enough?" Austin hissed in his ear. Digging his fingers into Cam's hips, he pulled out only to shove his cock back in. *Tight. Slick.* "Goddamn, I love this ass." He watched with unmistakable hunger in his eyes how his erection slid in and out of Cam. Unfortunately, he knew he wasn't going to last long, so he wrapped his fingers around Cam's hard cock and stroked him as he fucked his way toward climax.

Cam's head lolled back against Austin's shoulder, and he

turned for a kiss. Austin obliged and stole his breath.

"I need to come," Cam groaned breathlessly. "Fuck, I need—"

"I'll get you there." Austin's hands went back to Cam's hips, and he pushed him forward a little. "One hand on the wall," he commanded. "You know what to do with the other." He rammed into Cam's ass and gritted his teeth. Over and over. It had to hurt, but Cam moaned for more, and it wasn't long before they surrendered to their orgasms. "Fuck, Cam!" Austin threw his head back, his hips instinctively shifting forward in jerky movements. In hot pulses, his release filled Cam's ass. His chest heaved and every muscle tensed.

Cam clenched his jaw, releasing stream after stream against the tiled wall.

For several moments afterward, they could only hear the rushing water and their labored breaths.

"If you wanna carry me to bed, I probably won't stop you," Cam said after a while, still breathing heavily. "My poor ass."

Austin chuckled and began to wash them up. "You fucking begged for it." At Cam's tired groan and weak nod, he laughed and squeezed Cam affectionately. "Come on, baby. Let's finish up here and go to bed."

EPILOGUE

Two years later...

SLIPPING OUT OF the bedroom, Cam buttoned his khaki shorts and rolled up the sleeves of his white button-down. The thin leather cord around his wrist was still damp from his shower, and he grinned a little to himself, thinking back on this morning when Riley had given it to him for his thirty-sixth birthday. The three white beads with black letters that spelled out "car" made it a very special birthday present. Fitting for a mechanic, Riley had said, but then she'd finished with, "You gotta explain to everyone that it stands for Cam, Austin, and Riley, though. Peoples gotta know that."

Cam was gonna make sure that *peoples* knew.

As he passed the living room, he stopped short when he saw Riley and a friend of hers dancing to some fucking awful pop

x

239

music. But it wasn't the music that horrified Cam; it was the fact that these two twelve-year-old girls were shaking parts they didn't even have yet.

"What the hell are you doing?" he practically shouted.

"We're dancing!" Riley laughed, shaking her butt in some summer dress Lily had bought her. "Duh!"

"That's not dancing." Cam was irritated. "Unless you're over eighteen and there's a pole," he bitched under his breath. *Over my dead body.* "Listen to me, sweetheart." He walked over and held out his hand. Riley took it with a curious expression on her face. "First of all, when a motherfu—a boy... asks you to dance, you only say yes if he kisses the top of your hand first." He held both hers and kissed her knuckles. "That means he's a good guy. Got it?" Riley giggled and nodded. Her friend, Mya, was giggling, too. "And when you dance alone, just you or with your girlfriends, you stick to the chicken dance. Are we clear?"

The two girls nearly bowled over in laughter, but Cam didn't see what was so fucking funny.

"Lame!" Mya exclaimed.

"Yeah—that's for kids!" Riley agreed.

"Like you'd know what's lame." Cam scoffed and turned toward the kitchen. "You're twelve!" Reaching the kitchen where Austin was busy unpacking the catered side dishes for today's barbecue, Cam sighed and grabbed a beer from the fridge. "Have you seen what's goin' on in there?"

Austin shook his head, though not as if to say no. "I'm thinking about shipping that kid off to a convent." He gave Cam a quick once-over and stepped closer. "You look good." So did

Austin, in Cam's opinion, in his cargo shorts and black T-shirt. "Did I tell you that my parents are taking Riley tonight?"

Cam smirked and slipped his fingers into Austin's belt, tugging him close enough for them to touch. "A couple times." He slid his nose along Austin's clean-shaven jaw, a low groan rumbling in his chest. "And you like to remind me." He pressed his pelvis against Austin's, which earned him a quiet moan. "You just wanna stuff my mouth with your dick." With a husky chuckle, he placed Austin's hand on his crotch. "But I think it's my turn tonight, baby." He was dying to get Austin's mouth on him, and then he wanted a raw fucking in return. Cam's ass clenched at the thought of having Austin inside him. It had been *days*...

"Damn," Austin muttered gruffly. "So not the time." He adjusted himself and backed off. "Go check the grill or something. Our families and friends will be here any minute."

Cam laughed quietly and when he got to the living room again, the two girls were now watching TV, though the music was still on.

"We're visiting my little brother at camp tomorrow," Mya was saying as they watched some skinny models on the flat screen. "You wanna come with?"

"Sounds like fun," Riley said. "Just have to ask my dads first."

Cam's eyes grew large. One word went on repeat in his head, and the loop circled his goddamn heart. *Dads, dads, dads, dads.* As in two of them. Not only Austin. Cam, too. Abruptly, he spun on his heel and returned to the kitchen. While Riley had always been accepting of him and liked him as her father's partner, it felt fucking glorious to hear that he was so fully included in her family.

"The grill ready?" Austin asked distractedly.

Cam didn't say a word; he couldn't. He just walked up to Austin and pulled him in for a bruising kiss.

"Umph." Austin was taken aback by the force.

Making sure the kiss didn't end, Cam pinned him to the fridge and pushed his tongue into Austin's mouth. Inside of him, he grew impatient by the lack of words. He felt like he needed to say something about what he'd just heard, but it was too soon. In true Cam fashion, he got annoyed, but because words continued to fail him, he kissed Austin some more. On his lips, his jaw, his cheeks, his neck—until they were both out of breath and hard.

"We should g-get married," he blurted out, closing his eyes.

Fuck. That had not been smooth.

"Are you serious right now?" Austin was breathing heavily against Cam's neck. "I can't *believe*—you just…"

"Yeah," he rasped. His shoulders tensed up, and he was ready to get defensive. It was what he did. He braced himself. "You got a problem with that?"

Austin exhaled a shaky laugh and lifted his head. His eyes shone with… something. Cam was too high-strung and anxious to read into it, but it reminded him of the time last year when he'd added Austin's and Riley's birthdates to his collection of tattoos.

Just the day after, Austin had made an appointment for his very first tattoo, which now sat on his shoulder blade. It was Riley's handprint from when she was little to represent his daughter, and the words, "To hell and back with you," underneath it to represent Cam.

"Check my left pocket, baby," Austin whispered, bringing

Cam's hand to the pocket in question.

Still tense, Cam avoided eye contact, fixating on a point behind Austin's shoulder, and acted on autopilot. He dug his hand down into the pocket, only to brush his fingers against two metal objects. Circular ones.

Austin smiled carefully and touched their foreheads together. "I was going to ask you tonight when everyone had left."

"Oh," Cam uttered dumbly. "I came unprepared." He slowly pulled away his hand again. "I can buy the rings when we get hitched, though." He needed to shut the fuck up. *Christ.*

His dad also wore two rings, and he liked the idea of having one for engagement and one for marriage. So… now he wanted to get that first one on his finger.

"All I want is your yes," Austin murmured. Sticking his hand into his pocket, he retrieved the two gold bands that lay in his open palm.

"You have it. Of course." Cam nodded. "Yeah." His gaze remained on the rings, finding eye contact difficult right now. He watched as Austin slid the ring on his left ring finger, then swallowed hard against the emotions when a matching ring ended up on Austin's. "I love you," he muttered, only lifting his gaze to Austin's mouth.

"I love you, too." Austin tilted his head down a couple inches and pressed his warm lips to Cam's.

Austin's tattoo said it all. They'd been to hell and back together; they'd waded through feelings and obstacles in the aftermath, never leaving the other's side. Maybe things weren't perfect. Cam still needed to sleep with the bedroom door open, and Austin kept tempering his anger issues by pushing his physical limits on a punching bag, in a pool, or while running. Cam enjoyed having family over these days, as long as he wasn't too crowded. Riley wasn't allowed to wake up Cam in the mornings, for fear of startling him. Austin still tended to downplay his own struggles, but he was working on it. Gale would be in their lives for years to come, and some scars would never fade.

But Cam and Austin stuck together, gun or no gun, and created their own little piece of fucking awesome in that house in Bakersfield.

As friends, lovers, partners, brothers-in-arms, and with Riley, as a family.

CHASE AND REMY'S STORY
Outcome, sequel to Aftermath

THREE YEARS AGO, Chase Gallardo ran toward freedom with his fellow survivors after having spent five months in captivity. He hasn't stopped running since. Only now, it's the memories he's constantly trying to escape. Haunting echoes of a man who forced Chase to play the part of another, the kidnapper's younger brother. Chase may have survived, but that doesn't mean he's really living. Until one day, when his employee tells him there's a man sitting at the bar, wearing only underwear.

Remy Stahl has given up—almost. For a year, alcohol, drugs, and faces without names have kept him company. But he has two friends who refuse to give up on him, and they lock him up in his house in an attempt to save him from himself. Though, never underestimate an addict's desire to see the bottom of another bottle. Remy escapes, and he doesn't give a rat's ass that he's nearly naked.

This is the sequel to Aftermath, where Cam and Austin met, struggled, and fell in love. Outcome takes us back to Bakersfield— and the characters we know—with Chase and Remy's story. Fueled by anger, guilt, and shame, they're not off to an easy start.

ACKNOWLEDGEMENTS

Lisa at *Silently Correcting Your Grammar*. Friend and personal *consiglieri* first and foremost, editor second, and always Boss Lady. I can't even imagine where I would've been today if it weren't for you, and I don't want to! Thank you for everything you do and for the amazing friend you are.

J. I don't know how people can shack up with writers, but I'm eternally grateful that you put up with it. When I close myself in, disappear in to fiction, work all night, go to bed when you come home, and forget to eat, you're patiently waiting for the frenzy to settle. You know things will calm down as soon as the next project is published, and you know it's a rinse and repeat kind of deal. Yet, you stick around. It's the money, isn't it?

Emma and Meurinne, for giving Austin and Cam careers. Emma, who also happens to be my little sister, is the kick-ass mechanic behind Cam, and she did an excellent job of making me look like a question mark when she got passionate about engines, makes, and... *stuff*. What's so wrong about calling an engine a thingamabob, huh? Meurinne did well, too! After telling everything she knew about the accounting business and providing me endless lists of information, correct terminology, and... *stuff*... Austin knew what he was doing, but I sure didn't. Thank you, ladies!

Lisa Two, or L2 for short. Thank you for beta reading and giving me the second perspective I needed!

Last but not least, every reader who told me to turn my hobby into a career and publish. See? I can obey, and now I owe all of you!

More from Cara Dee at *www.caradeewrites.com*

Made in the USA
Lexington, KY
20 April 2015